MALIBU MUSIC

Gerry had promised Bianca that their friendship would be platonic. But for how long could a man like Gerry keep such a promise? And what was it he was hiding from her?

Books you will enjoy
by ROSEMARY HAMMOND

TWO DOZEN RED ROSES

It was part of Sarah's job as Sloan Sheridan's secretary to send two dozen red roses to his cast-off girlfriends. But there was no way she was ever going to find herself on the receiving end of that kind of dismissal! So, as Sloan still believed her to be a married woman, it seemed prudent to let him go on thinking it . . .

THE HABIT OF LOVING

Matthew Stratton and Paula Waring had joined forces to stop the political hostesses of Washington trying to marry them off. But then Paula read a gossip column, and Matthew suggested a more permanent joining—in a marriage of convenience . . .

MALIBU MUSIC

BY

ROSEMARY HAMMOND

MILLS & BOON LIMITED
15–16 BROOK'S MEWS
LONDON W1A 1DR

First published in Great Britain 1985
by Mills & Boon Limited

This edition 1985

ISBN 0 263 75180 5

Set in Monophoto Times 11 on 11 pt.
05–1085 – 51053

Made and printed in Great Britain by
Richard Clay (The Chaucer Press) Ltd,
Bungay, Suffolk

CHAPTER ONE

BIANCA JAMESON set down the priceless violin, the thousand-dollar bow, closed the score of the Brahms concerto and started to pace from one end to the other of the vast living room in her parents' apartment.

She was close to tears, but Jamesons didn't cry, she reminded herself, and squared her shoulders. At the window she looked down at the bleak January landscape. Most of the trees in Central Park were bare, and down below on Fifth Avenue the crowds of pedestrians scurried forward with their heads bent down against the icy wind, their coat collars turned up, necks muffled with woollen scarves, their booted feet crunching on the frozen pavement.

New York in winter, Bianca thought, was a sight to make her depressed state even worse. The last snowfall had been a week ago, and the temperature had stayed below freezing ever since. Now the soft pristine white had turned a hard dingy grey, piled up and frozen solid along the curbs of the street, the paths through the park.

She sighed and made herself turn back to the music stand. Her spirits sank even lower. She couldn't face it. It was no use trying. Her fingers wouldn't move properly on the frets, the tempo was all wrong, her pitch bad. What was worse, she couldn't *feel* the music. One note followed another in a meaningless jumble of sounds every time she tried.

She gazed around the beautiful room which had been her home for as long as she could remember. Her home, that is, when the family was in New York and not following her father around the world in one of his conducting tours.

A small, cheerless fire flickered in the fireplace. She never had learned to make a proper fire. Over the mantel hung a portrait of her father painted by her talented sister, Laura. There were photographs of the rest of the family scattered about the room on tables: her oldest brother, Nick, at the piano, playing with the Chicago symphony orchestra; Tony, her other older brother, straddling his cello surrounded by the three other members of the prestigious Orion string quartet; her sister, Norma, dressed as Cio Cio San, making her triumphant debut at the Met in *Madame Butterfly*.

We all look alike, Bianca thought desperately, catching sight of her reflection in the ornate gilt-framed mirror over the sideboard. We all have the same dark hair and eyes, thin rather intense face and straight nose. Why, then, am I the only one without talent? Why do I have to be the only failure in the family?

The telephone shrilled loudly, cutting into the utter stillness of the apartment like a fire alarm. She jumped, then ran into the hall to answer it. It was her sister, Laura, calling from her home in California.

'How are you getting along there all by yourself?' came the cheerful voice.

Too cheerful, Bianca thought. Laura, although next to her in age, was still eleven years older and, like the rest of the family, insisted on treating her like the baby who still needed protection and checking on from time to time.

'Fine. Just fine.' Bianca tried to put a little spark into her voice. Yesterday her mother calling from Paris, today Laura from California, clear across the country. The family grapevine was still in fine working order, she thought drily.

'Good, good,' came her sister's hearty voice. 'How's the Brahms coming? Think you'll be ready to knock 'em dead up in Boston?'

She must know, Bianca thought. She could well imagine her mother's frantic call to Laura after their strained conversation yesterday. With both parents in Paris, Tony in London, Norma in Milan and Nick in Buenos Aires, Laura would be pressed into service to take care of little sister just because she happened to be in the same country.

Might as well tell the truth, Bianca decided. Surely she already knows. 'I'm thinking of cancelling the concert,' she muttered defensively. 'I'm just not ready. I went over all this yesterday with Mother. I'm just not ready,' she repeated, and was horrified to hear how her voice wobbled. She dreaded the family's pity.

'Well,' Laura said after a short silence, 'that's okay, Bianca. There's no law that says you have to do it. You're young.'

Sure, Bianca thought bitterly. I'm young. Only twenty-two. At that age Norma was already singing small parts professionally, Laura had had her first one-man show, and Nick and Tony were playing with major orchestras. Child prodigies, all of them. Except me.

'No, there's no law,' Bianca agreed. She ran a hand through her short unruly mop of dark hair. 'Just Jameson's law.'

'What's that?' Laura asked lightly.

'Oh, you know. Accomplishment. Success. Ambition.'

'Forget that,' Laura said firmly. 'That's a myth, and it isn't why I called anyway. Listen, I've received an offer from the Slade in London to teach there for a year.'

'Oh, Laura, that's exciting,' Bianca said in a rush, genuinely glad for her sister. 'But won't it interfere with your own work?' Laura was a highly successful portrait painter with a thriving clientele among wealthy Southern Californians.

'Not really,' came the reply. 'I've been thinking about giving up portraits and trying something more impressionistic anyway. This will give me a chance to experiment with my own work and still have the security of a paying job.'

'It sounds like a perfect opportunity for you,' Bianca said, her black mood gone. 'What will you do about your house while you're gone?'

'Well, that's the main reason I'm calling.' There was a short pause. 'You probably know Mother called me from Paris yesterday,' she went on cautiously.

'I guessed as much,' Bianca replied in a dry tone. 'Listen, I appreciate everyone's concern, but I do get a little tired of my role as the problem child of the family. I'm a big girl now. I'll be okay. I'm just a little—I don't know—burnt out, I guess, trying too hard to keep up with the rest of you. I think I want a rest, to get away from music for a while.'

'Darling, you are *not* the problem child of the family. We love you, silly, and only want what's best for you. And I think you're very wise to take a little vacation from your music. When Mother told me about your—your burnout, if that's what you want to call it, the whole thing fell into place.'

'What are you getting at?' Bianca asked cautiously.

'I don't want to lease my house,' Laura went on excitedly. 'These Hollwood acidheads would tear it to pieces. But I can't just leave it vacant. I want you to come out here and stay in it for the year I'm away in London.'

A warm glow, a flood of relief washed over Bianca. California. Sunshine. Her sister's charming house on the beach at Malibu. It sounded like heaven.

'Are you there, Bianca?' came Laura's worried voice after a few moments.

'Yes, I'm here,' Bianca breathed at last. 'When do you want me to come?'

She could hear Laura's audible sigh of relief over the wire and thought, so what if it is just charity? At this point I'll take whatever crumbs she wants to throw my way.

'How about Wednesday?' came the prompt reply. 'Is that too soon? Today is Monday. I have to leave Friday. I can pick you up at the airport.'

'No. That's not too soon. I'll call right away for reservations and let you know when the plane arrives.'

'Good. That's all settled, then. See you Wednesday.'

Two days later, Bianca was on a plane winging her way across the country. By the time they touched down at the airport it was late afternoon, the western sun barely visible through the thick covering of smog.

Smog or not, Bianca thought, as she strode

along with the other passengers into the terminal, at least it was sunshine. Even in January, Los Angeles was balmy compared to the frozen East Coast. Her red woollen suit was a perfect choice for the temperature, which was cool, but not bitterly cold, certainly far above the freezing weather in New York.

Laura was waiting for her at the baggage counter. She was dressed casually, Southern California style, in jeans, white turtleneck jumper and a good-looking tweed hacking jacket. At the sight of her sister's familiar face, Bianca felt the tears sting her eyes, and she ran to embrace her, clinging to her solid, comforting warmth.

Laura pushed her back a little after a few moments and held her at arms' length, giving her a long penetrating look as though to assess her true condition.

'You look terrible,' she stated flatly at last.

'Thanks a lot.' Bianca gave her a weak smile. 'That helps my morale considerably.'

'Sorry,' Laura said briskly. 'You know me. Heart of gold and foot in mouth. Let's get your baggage and get out of this rotten smog. At least at the beach the air is clear.'

When they had collected Bianca's two large suitcases, they walked down to the car park where Laura's little red BMW was installed.

'I see you've brought your fiddle,' Laura remarked casually as she stowed Bianca's baggage in the trunk of the car.

Bianca glanced down at the black violin case she had carried with her on the plane. She had fully intended to leave it behind when she'd left the apartment that morning, but at the last minute she had changed her mind. Not only was the instrument too valuable to leave in the untenanted apartment, but she felt almost naked without it.

She made a face. 'Yes,' she said shortly. 'It's like an albatross. If the parents hadn't paid so much money for it, sometimes I think I'd like to toss it in the ocean.'

They got into the car and Laura started the engine. 'Why don't you just sell it and be done with it, then?' she asked as she edged her way into the freeway traffic.

Bianca stared fixedly down at her hands in her lap. 'I don't know,' she mumbled. 'Guilt. Fear. Hope.'

'Guilt about what? Hope for what?'

Bianca shook her head miserably. She glanced at her sister's profile, so like her own, yet with so much more confidence in the determined lift of the chin. The dark eyes were fixed firmly on the road ahead as she wove expertly in and out of the heavy traffic. There was a little smudge of paint on her forehead, another on her strong brown hand.

'I'm sorry, Laura,' she said at last, 'to be such a drag. I know I'm whining, and I hate that. Let's forget about me. The California sunshine will cure whatever ails me in time. Tell me about your new job.'

She forced a smile and tried to concentrate all her attention on her sister's excited plans for her year in London. She wanted to rejoice with her. She was honestly happy for her. There had never been any jealousy in the family. Each member was encouraged to develop their own gifts, but was always ready to admire the others' accomplishments.

Bianca loved her family with all her heart and was intensely proud of their considerable successes in the fields they had chosen. When Norma made her debut at the Met, Bianca had been in the family box, cheering loudly for her sister's beautiful soprano voice. When Nick had cut his first solo recording, she had run out and bought ten copies to give to friends. She tried to attend as many of Tony's quartet's performances as possible, and was their most ardent fan.

No, she thought, half-listening to Laura as they drove along, I'm not jealous. I just wish . . . What do I wish? she asked herself. The honest answer was that she wished she didn't feel she had to keep up with them. She was only partly joking when she told Laura she'd like to throw her violin in the ocean. She enjoyed playing it, but she hated the competition, the constant striving for achievement.

The truth was, however, that having been born into such a talented family, there seemed to be no other recourse for her. How would she live without the unremitting struggle for artistic success? No other life seemed possible. It was heresy to even consider giving it up.

She just needed a rest, she told herself, that's all. A few months of sunshine and solitude and she'd be ready to tackle her career again in earnest. She wouldn't rush things. After all, she was a serious musician. She just hadn't been ready, emotionally, mentally, musically, for the concert in Boston and had been right to cancel it.

They were driving due west now on the coast towards Malibu. The sun had just set, leaving a reddish glow over the horizon and lighting the blue of the ocean with a golden path. There was a slight breeze, a few whitecaps on the water, and the air smelled fresh and clean after the oppressive haze of the interior.

The wide boulevard was lined with beach houses, some opulent mansions with a stark modern architecture, others smaller, more old-fashioned, with the typical red-tiled roof and stucco exterior of Southern California homes. Tall, ungainly palm trees were set in rows on either side of the road, and in the front gardens, bright geraniums and roses still bloomed in the mild climate.

Laura's house was one of the older beach cottages, but in the five years she had lived there she had done extensive remodelling, so that it had become, inside and out, a unique expression of her own vivid personality.

The BMW pulled now into a wide paved area just off the road. They got out of the car and walked towards the front door.

'Well, here we are,' Laura said, unlocking the door. 'Home, sweet home. I'll miss it.'

'I don't blame you,' Bianca said. 'I can't get over the flowers blooming in January. It seems almost sinful.'

Laura laughed as she led the way down a wide flight of stairs to the main level of the house. The whole rear wall was glass and looked out on to the sea. Just outside was a wide wooden verandah set up on heavy wooden support beams above the sandy beach, and another narrow staircase led down from the far edge to the beach. Beyond was the wide expanse of the Pacific Ocean.

Bianca opened the sliding glass door and went out on to the verandah. Leaning against the railing, she stood there for several moments listening to the pounding surf as the giant foamy waves broke on the shore, and drinking in the salty tang of the evening air. A few gulls still scavenged along the tidewater line, screeching and scolding each other, and in the distance she saw a family of sandpipers strolling nonchalantly up the deserted beach.

She knew she had done the right thing to come. Already, her heart was more at peace, her jangled nerves calmer, her confused mind more rested than they had been for months. The sea and the solitude and the sunshine will heal me, she thought, and in a year I'll know what I must do.

Early Friday morning, Bianca deposited Laura at the airport, bade her a tearful goodbye, then drove back to the beach in the BMW with a sense of joy and liberation.

She checked the mailbox before she went inside the house. The middle one was Laura's and had Jameson printed on it in bold black letters. The one on the left looked newly painted, with the name Richards scrawled lightly on it with a felt-tipped pen; the one on the right had the name Emory in neat block letters. Laura had told her that the Emorys were an elderly retired couple who kept to themselves, and that the house on the left was vacant, its occupants in Japan for several months. This meant that there would be virtually no neighbours at all with whom she'd have to share the stretch of beach. This suited her purposes perfectly.

It was cooler today, slightly overcast and with a brisk breeze stirring up the whitecaps on the ocean. After a light lunch, Bianca put a heavy Aran turtleneck sweater on over her cotton shirt and jeans and went down for a walk on the beach.

The breeze was much stronger down here by the water, and she found herself wishing she had worn a scarf or cap on her head. The wind blew her short dark curls in every direction, and she shivered as she walked along, her hands in the pockets of the jeans, her thin shoulders hunched forward.

The roar of the ocean and the loud screeching of the gulls filled her ears, and soon a light spattering of rain began to beat against her face. She was tousled, cold and beginning to get wet, but as she trudged forward far up the empty beach, she felt better than she had in months, freer, more light-hearted.

It isn't just the sunshine that's going to heal me, she thought contentedly as she lifted her face into the wind and rain, but this sense of liberation, this beautiful solitariness, where there's no competing, no struggle to achieve. A few weeks of this and I'll *want* to play again, she thought.

Thoroughly soaked by now, she decided it was time she went back to the house. She had walked far down to the left, and as she retraced her steps, the wind at her back now, she glanced up at the bluff to her right, curious about Laura's neighbours.

The house immediately next door was a large imposing modernistic structure, all wood and glass, that jutted out precariously over the bluff, supported by cantilevered beams. There wasn't a sign of life. Light-coloured curtains were drawn across the expanse of glass that faced the sea. These were the people who were in Japan, she thought, and wondered how long they'd be away. It was foolish to leave such an obviously expensive house vacant, but for her own sake she hoped it would be a long time before they came back.

* * *

During the next few weeks Bianca's days gradually settled into a natural and pleasant routine. In the mornings she shopped for groceries and did all her household chores. After lunch, she took long walks up and down the beach, which she had virtually to herself. It was still too cool for swimmers or sunbathers. In the evenings she built a fire in the living room and either listened to music or read.

The weather remained blustery and damp, and now when she went down to the beach she wore a cap on her head and a waterproof jacket over her sweater. There was little heavy rain, as a rule, and even at its coldest, the climate was tropical compared to New York.

She was eating well and sleeping like the dead. She knew that soon she would start practising again, not because she had to, but because she would want to. Several times she had taken her violin out of its case and run her hands over the smooth, mellow, old wood, and she realised that it was only a matter of time before she wouldn't be able to resist tuning it and trying it out again.

It was so quiet in this part of Malibu, with only the roaring of the surf and muffled traffic noises coming occasionally from the road up above the house to break the stillness. Once in a while on her hikes she would run into other solitary walkers or joggers, but they rarely spoke to her beyond a brief, polite greeting.

One night, however, after she'd been living in Laura's house for about two weeks, she was awakened out of a sound sleep by an insistent blare of loud music. She sat bolt upright in bed, her heart pounding, her mind disorientated by the sudden, unexpected intrusion into the quiet night, and looked around the darkened room.

Had she inadvertently left on the stereo set? She listened carefully. No, not only did the sounds seem to be coming from outside, but she would never have put on music like that, a strident, pounding rock beat that hurt her musical sensibilities as much as her ears.

She jumped out of bed and ran down the hall and through the living room to the wooden verandah. When she slid the glass door open, the intensity of the music hit her in an explosion of raucous sound. She went out on to the deck and stood leaning on the railing, peering out at the darkened beach below, thinking perhaps the music might be coming from midnight picnickers with a loud transistor radio.

Then, out of the corner of her eye, her attention was caught by an unfamiliar sight. She turned and saw that the house next door was ablaze with light. Shivering in the cool night air, dressed only in flannel pyjamas, she hugged herself tightly and stared. The curtains had been pulled open, and she could see several people milling about inside the house and out on the wide verandah.

Suddenly the music stopped, and she could hear loud voices raised in laughter and shouted conversations. It must be a party, she thought groggily, still dazed from her deep sleep. But no one lived there. Should she call the police? Perhaps a gang of kids had broken in. She hesitated, not sure what she should do.

She gazed out into the darkness, trying to get a better look at the people. But the house was too far away, at least a hundred feet, and all she could make out were dim, moving shapes. There did seem to be a lot of them, and although they were very loud, there was no sign of violence or sound of breakage.

Then the music came on again, a slower tune this time, one she recognised as having been very popular a few years ago. Like most serious musicians, Bianca could enjoy almost any form of music that wasn't merely a brutal assault on the senses, and in a few moments she found herself humming along with the lead singer.

Finally, she decided she'd better just mind her own business and leave them alone. Possibly the tenants had come back from Japan and were throwing a welcome home party. She went inside, locked the door carefully behind her just in case, and went back to bed. Maybe she'd find out more tomorrow.

The next day on her afternoon walk, when she passed by the house, she gazed up at it with a new sense of curiosity and interest, but it was exactly the same as it had always been, the curtains drawn shut, utterly still and silent, and seemingly uninhabited.

She walked slowly towards it, closer than she ever had before, and stood for a long time staring up at the odd structure that seemed to be hanging in space, a puzzled frown on her face. There was absolutely no sign of life. Nothing seemed to be broken or out of place. Soon after she'd gone back to bed last night—it was not quite two o'clock—the noise had ceased as abruptly as it had started.

Had she dreamt the whole episode? No, that was impossible. She remembered it quite clearly. It had been real. Had someone broken in? She stood there, wondering whether she should climb the steep wooden staircase from the beach up to the verandah to investigate.

She had just about decided that she would, when the wide expanse of curtains were suddenly pulled open, and she found herself gazing up at a figure framed in the window. Quickly, instinctively, embarrassed at being caught goggling like that, she turned and hurried away up the beach. But not before she had received a clear glimpse of a tall dark man dressed only in very brief white jockey shorts.

With her cheeks flaming, even in the cool breeze, she bent her head and plunged forward, not daring to look back. Had he seen her? She was glad she'd worn her windbreaker and woollen cap. It constituted a sort of disguise.

On her way home, half an hour later, when she passed by the house next door, she hunched her shoulders forward and kept her eyes averted. If he was still there, she didn't want to see him. There had been something faintly menacing about that tall solitary figure standing at the window, virtually naked, and Bianca's pleasant peaceful existence seemed oddly shattered by the mere brief glimpse she'd had of him.

She picked up an armload of driftwood and kindling from the protected storage cupboard on Laura's verandah on her way into the house, and, miracle of miracles, after soaking for half an hour in a warm tub, she did manage to get a respectable fire burning. Maybe the porous wood, bleached white by the sun, burned more easily, she thought as she sat drying her hair in front of the steady blaze.

She had put some music on the stereo set, a recording Tony's group had recently made of Schubert's Trout Quintet, with her brother, Nick, at the piano. As the lilting, rippling strains poured into the room, Bianca felt a new surge of pride at both her brothers' fine artistry.

The telephone rang. She turned down the volume on the stereo and went into the bedroom to answer it.

'Bianca?' came a masculine voice. 'Is this Bianca Jameson?'

'Yes, it is,' she replied cautiously. The voice was vaguely familiar to her, but she couldn't quite place it. It wasn't Tony or Nick or her father, and no one else even knew she was here.

'It's Tom. Tom Schiffren.'

Bianca tightened up and scowled at the telephone. Her family was at it again. She deeply resented this intrusion into the solitary world she was enjoying so much.

'How are you, Tom?' she said stiffly. 'I thought you were in Paris.'

Tom was the concertmaster of the orchestra her father was touring with and had been her teacher and coach for many years. What was he doing in California? Surely her family wouldn't go to such lengths to check on her? She'd only been here a few weeks.

'The orchestra finished up the Paris engagement, and we all came home. Your father is going on to Budapest as guest conductor.'

'What are you doing in California, Tom? Just passing through?' She was still suspicious.

He laughed. 'Hardly. No. Some time ago I was offered a job on the faculty of the music department at UCLA. I'm a California resident as of yesterday.'

'I see,' she said slowly. 'That's wonderful, Tom.' She was torn between genuine liking for the man who had taught her so much and her desire to be left alone.

'How about you?' he asked. 'Still working hard and practising like a good girl?'

'I'm taking a little vacation from playing,' she said carefully, then, feeling guilty, she added lightly, 'But I do intend to keep up on my practising, teacher.'

He chuckled. 'That's good.' There was a short, uncomfortable silence. Then, his voice low and cautious, he went on. 'I heard you cancelled out of the Boston concert.'

'Yes,' she said shortly. 'I wasn't ready.'

'Hey, Bianca, it's okay. Not to worry. It happens to all of us, and sometimes even the most dedicated musician just has to get away from it for a while. You're too good to give it up altogether, though. I hope you realise that.'

'No,' she said. 'I won't ever give it up, although I'm not sure I'll ever pursue solo performing again. I don't think I have the right temperament for it. You're right, though. I did need to get out from under the pressure for a while.'

'Good. Well, I just wanted to let you know I was in the area and available to help when you decide you're ready for some coaching.' He paused. 'I won't push, Bianca, but I would like to see you.'

'Maybe later on, Tom. Right now I'm really enjoying just being by myself. There are some things I have to sort out.'

'Sure, I understand.' He gave her his phone number. 'Call me if you need anything. Later on maybe we can have dinner or go to a concert. You might like to visit my studio here at the university. I've got some fine students, and the set-up is fantastic.'

'Yes, I'd like that. Thanks so much for calling, Tom. It's good to talk to you again.'

They said goodbye then, and Bianca walked slowly back to the fire. It had been good to hear a familiar voice, but she was relieved that he seemed to understand her need to be alone. She'd call him in a few weeks.

At one time, when Bianca was a gawky teenager, she'd had a violent crush on Tom Schiffren. Because of her family's intense dedication to art, her formative years had been extremely sheltered, almost abnormally so. While other girls her age were going out on dates, she was practising scales. It had seemed like a perfectly normal situation to her at the time. Her brothers and sisters had been raised the same way, almost as monks and nuns, with singleminded dedication to their chosen work.

The schoolgirl crush on Tom had been an embarrassment to him as well as to her family, and when it was over, she had been terribly ashamed of the stupid things she had said and done to attract his attention. Miraculously, they had ended up good friends and, ultimately, the experience strengthened Bianca's commitment to cultivate her musical gift.

The next few days were warm and balmy, and Bianca began to make full use of the wide verandah for sunbathing. She sat out there in the late afternoon when the sun was hottest and before the evening breeze began to blow. Her pale skin was beginning to tan from the exposure. She felt wonderful and knew that soon she would succumb to her own instincts and start practising again. Then she would call Tom.

She also began taking her walks in the opposite

direction and had met the Emorys, a frail elderly couple who welcomed her to the community and issued a vague invitation to stop by for tea some afternoon. She still hadn't seen any more sign of life from the other house, and when she asked the Emorys about the tenants, they had looked vaguely at each other, then at her, and said that they didn't even know they had gone to Japan.

After a few days, she began to think she was being silly to avoid that whole stretch of beach to the left on the slim chance that she would encounter the man in the window. Whoever he was, he seemed to be gone by now anyway.

CHAPTER TWO

AFTER a lovely week of blessed sun, Bianca woke up one morning to an overcast sky and the threat of a storm in the air. Too bad, she thought, as she dressed in jeans and heavy sweater again. She had enjoyed the warm weather and had hoped she could discard her heavier clothing for good.

She stood at the kitchen counter now, eating her breakfast of toast and coffee and gazing out the window at the grey, dismal day. It was still only early February, she thought philosophically, and the Emorys had mentioned that it would be April before the weather stabilised into the famous consistent Californian sunshine.

Right after breakfast she went out on the verandah to get more firewood and sweep a little before it started to rain, but when she opened the glass door a sudden gust of wind struck her. The sea was churning with whitecaps, the tide breaking violently on the shore, and out on the horizon there was a bank of black clouds moving in fast.

Not a good day to be out, she thought. She quickly gathered up an armload of wood and was just about to go back inside the house when she heard a faint crying sound coming from underneath the verandah. She stopped, listening carefully for a moment, and then she heard it again.

It had started to rain, a light spattering now, but soon there would be a deluge. She ran inside to get on her cap and windbreaker, then harried back to the railing and leaned over the side.

Then she saw it. There, under cover of the overhanging verandah, sat a little black kitten, its nose lifted in the air, mewing loudly and pitifully. With a cry of alarm, Bianca started down the stairs, intent on rescuing it, but before she reached the bottom, she was startled by the sound of loud barking coming from the beach. She looked up to see a large golden-haired dog come bounding up towards the house, obviously bent on routing the little cat, who had turned to face the intruder, hissing and spitting, its skinny back arched against him.

'Oh, no,' Bianca cried. She flew down the last few steps brandishing the broom she still held in her hands, ready to fight him off if she had to, and calling, 'Shoo, shoo,' loudly at him.

The dog continued yapping and dancing wildly, kicking up great sprays of wet sand, but after a few moments, Bianca realised that he was only a pup, albeit a very large one, and seemed to be more playful than dangerous.

Apartment-bred, Bianca had little experience of animals, but she sensed from the way the excited dog was wagging its long, plumed tail and crouching down on its front paws, that in his canine mind, anyway, the encounter with the black cat was more a game than the outbreak of hostilities.

Still wary, Bianca continued to hold the broom up defensively in front of her as she began cautiously to move towards the brave little kitten, whose pure black coat bristled on end with fury.

Then, with all her concentration fixed on the two animals, she dimly heard a man's voice calling from the shore.

'Hey, kid, put that damn broom down, for God's sake. He won't hurt you.'

Startled, she obeyed instinctively, then looked in the direction of the voice. A tall dark-haired hatless man, dressed in jeans and heavy woollen jacket was striding towards her. She stood, open-mouthed, staring, the broom hanging loosely in her hands. It had to be him, she thought, the man in the window, and her face flamed hotly.

As he came towards her, he began to whistle shrilly and to call the dog. 'Come here, Barney,' came the firm command.

But Barney, caught up in the joy of the game, ignored him completely and continued barking and dancing, never, however, coming one inch closer to the snarling, hissing cat.

Bianca glared at the man. He glared back. He had reached the ecstatic dog by now and had a firm hold on his collar. He knelt down and snapped on a leather leash, patting the dog and scolding him at the same time for not obeying his earlier command.

Then he stood up and gave Bianca a withering glance. 'Listen, kid, don't you know a playful pup from a vicious dog? You should never threaten a barking dog that way, friendly or not.'

Kid! Who did he think she was, Bianca thought hotly, some juvenile delinquent who went around tormenting dumb animals?

'I wasn't going to hurt him,' she muttered in a low voice. Then, on the principle that the best defence was a good offence, she lifted her chin and said loudly, 'There's a leash law here in Malibu, you know. Dogs aren't allowed to run loose on the beach.' She wasn't sure about this, but it seemed logical.

The man frowned. His heavy dark eyebrows lowered and he took a step towards her, peering down at her in a long appraising look, his manner slightly menacing, so that Bianca had to make an effort not to back away from him.

'You're a girl,' he said at last in a surprised tone.

'Yes,' she snapped, still glaring.

'I had control of him,' he announced in a flat voice.

'Some control!' she said scornfully. 'I didn't notice him leaping obediently to your side when you called him.'

He continued to scowl at her, then suddenly he reached up to scratch his head and grinned broadly.

'You're right,' he admitted with a sigh of mock despair. 'I've spent a fortune and uncounted hours trying to get him obedience-trained, but he has a formidable mind of his own.'

Bianca found the smile totally disarming, and it suddenly dawned on her what an attractive man he was. He was heavily tanned, and his crisp shiny black hair was beautifully, professionally cut so that it waved thickly over his ears and forehead in a longish style. His eyes were dark, too, almost black, so heavily fringed with coal black lashes that they seemed hooded and oddly secretive. The cheekbones were high and prominent, and the smile on the wide full mouth was lazy, even faintly challenging.

To cover her confusion, Bianca turned away from him and marched over to the kitten, who was sitting calmly by a heavy post and daintily taking a bath. When she reached down to pick it up, the cat hissed and a black paw shot out and raked Bianca's hand painfully.

'Oh,' she cried, as she stared at her hand and saw blood ooze up from the long scratch marks, 'you ungrateful little beast!' She reached into her pocket for a tissue and while she dabbed at her bloody hand, she became painfully aware that the man was laughing.

She whirled around, then, ready to do battle, but the wide grin on his face was more friendly than mocking, and the anger drained out of her as suddenly as it came. Besides, the fickle kitten, having asserted its supremacy over everyone present, was now rubbing up against her leg, purring loudly, and when Bianca reached down cautiously to pick it up again, it fell limply into her arms, allowing itself to be held. Snuggling warmly on her shoulder now, it looked down triumphantly at the panting dog, who sat patiently by his master, firmly held in place by the restraining leash.

Then the man's eyes narrowed. 'What are you doing here, anyway?'

Bianca bristled, annoyed at the suspicious tone. 'I live here,' she snapped. Then she recalled the night of the party and her own suspicions. 'What are *you* doing here?'

He cocked his head to one side and gave her a cool look. 'I live here, too.' The dark head nodded briefly towards the house next door.

'I thought you were supposed to be in Japan,' she said warily.

'The owners are in Japan. They're friends of mine and are letting me use the house while they're away.'

The smiling, friendly manner was gone. He seemed almost hostile now, his voice curt, his face grim. Suddenly, without another word, he turned on his heel and started walking away from her, tugging at the leash so that the reluctant dog was forced to follow him.

After that, Bianca saw the strange man almost every day on the beach, and although they would nod briefly at each other in passing, they never spoke. He always had Barney with him, securely leashed now, and whenever the dog saw Bianca he would strain eagerly towards her. so that the man had to restrain him forcibly and pull him along.

Although she would have enjoyed making friends with the beautiful dog, Bianca was satisfied with the arrangement the way it was. Not only had she come to the beach to get away from people, but there was something disturbing about the man that warned her to keep him at a distance. His abrupt change of mood that day on the beach, from friendly amusement to almost hostile suspicion, puzzled her. She would have guessed from his manner that day that he was as reclusive as she was, except for the loud party that had awakened her that night.

One evening, a few weeks after the strange encounter on the beach, she took out her violin from the black case. After tuning it carefully at the piano, she tentatively played a few scales and arpeggios. Her fingers felt stiff and cramped as she tried to recapture some of her old technique, and she realised she'd better start practising in earnest or she'd lose her skill altogether.

It rained steadily for several days after that, and Bianca stayed inside practising in the afternoons now instead of walking. In a week her fingers had loosened considerably and she was almost able to play up to her old standard. Still, it was discouraging. She knew she was nowhere near ready to play professionally. She kept doggedly at it, however, comforting herself with the thought that at least she was heading in the right direction. When she was ready to tackle more difficult music, she would call Tom Schiffren for some of the coaching he had promised her. Perhaps he would know of a chamber music group that needed a violinist.

One evening, when she had just finished playing a difficult Pagannini *étude*, full of trills and double-bowing, there came a light rapping on the glass door to the verandah. Startled, she set the violin and bow down carefully on a chair and went to the door. It was pitch dark outside, and she had drawn the curtains shut.

'Who is it?' she called.'

'It's the dog-lover from next door,' came the cheerful reply.

Bianca hesitated. She had been so involved in her music lately that she had forgotten about him. What did he want? She switched on the outdoor light and pulled the curtains open. He was standing on the other side of the glass door, his hands in his trouser pockets and a friendly grin on his face. She unlocked the door and slid it open.

'What is it?' she asked.

'Can I come in?' When she hesitated, he raised his hands in the air. 'I'm harmless. Honest.'

Reluctantly, she slid the door open a little wider and stood aside to let him in. Although she wasn't really interested in his opinion of her, she was annoyed that he had caught her looking the way she did, with her hair tousled, an old pair of jeans and a baggy sweater on, and not a trace of make-up.

He stepped inside and slid the door shut behind him, then turned to face her. She stood by the window, her arms crossed in front of her, waiting impatiently for him to tell her what he wanted and leave. She didn't want to be rude, but something about him disturbed her, and she didn't at all like being here alone in the house with him at night. Who was he? She knew nothing about him.

He gave her a brief, slightly mocking look and sauntered casually into the living room. She stood and watched him with growing anger. He had a very self-confident walk, and Bianca found his whole proprietary air extremely annoying. He stopped now, facing away from her, his hands on his hips, legs apart, gazing around the room until his eyes lit on the violin.

He turned his head. 'Was that you playing?'

She took a step towards him, frowning. 'Yes, it was. Listen, was there something you wanted? I'm rather busy.'

He raised his heavy dark eyebrows, cocked his head to one side and gave her a disarming grin.

'Are you trying to get rid of me?' His tone was mocking and supremely confident.

She walked past him briskly and took up the violin to put it away. 'No. Of course not,' she said coolly, wrapping the instrument carefully in its red silk covering and placing it gently inside the black case. 'I'm just wondering why you're here.'

'I haven't seen you on the beach lately.'

'No. As I said, I've been busy.' She snapped the violin case shut and looked at him.

He shrugged. 'Just a neighbourly call. I was beginning to wonder if you were all right. My name is Gerry, by the way.' 'Gerry Richards. Spelled with a G.' He gave her an enquiring look.

'Bianca,' she said curtly. 'Bianca Jameson.'

He was silent for a moment, then, gazing at her coolly, appraisingly, he said at last, 'Listen, Bianca. I'm sorry if I was rude to you on the beach the other day.'

'Not at all,' she said politely.

'No, I mean it.' He was pacing around the room now, almost like a caged animal, his movements restless, as though he were looking for some clue to a puzzle. Bianca had the impression of immense contained energy in the way he moved and the flashing gleam in those almost black eyes. He unnerved her, and she wished again he would just go.

'Do you mind if I sit down?' he asked.

'Well, as a matter of fact . . .'

'Thanks,' he said, and sat down on the couch in front of the fireplace grinning up at her. 'So, Bianca, you're a musician.' He nodded affably towards the violin case. 'Are you any good?'

'Not very,' she said in a clipped tone.

He looked surprised. 'Really? You sounded great to me, although I admit I'm no judge.'

'No,' she bit out rudely, remembering the night of the party next door and the raucous blaring from the stereo. 'I don't imagine you are. I've heard your taste in music.'

He frowned then. 'Listen, I said I was sorry I was rude. Why the deep freeze? I'm just trying to be friendly.'

Bianca's rising anger began to spill over. Who did he think he was? Just the sight of him, sitting there as though he owned the place, infuriated her. Because *he* wanted company. Never mind what she wanted.

'You know, you've got a real nerve,' she said in

a heated tone. 'First of all you wake me up with your wild parties, then you yell at me like I'm some delinquent *boy*, then you ignore me for two weeks, and now you come barging in here wanting to be *neighbourly*, for heaven's sake.' Her voice rose wildly, her grey eyes flashed, and she was trembling with indignation. 'Well, I don't. I came here to be by myself, and I'd appreciate it if . . .'

'Hey,' he broke in, jumping to his feet. 'Calm down.' He grabbed her shoulders and shook her gently. 'What brought that on?'

She glared up at him. He was still grinning. 'What does it take,' she cried, 'to convince you to just leave me alone?'

His dark eyes were half-closed now, the mocking smile faintly threatening. 'You know,' he said in a low tone, 'you're very attractive when you're angry. Not at all like a boy.' His fingers began to knead her shoulders. 'You could use a little more weight, though.' His eyes travelled insolently down her thin body under the ill-fitting sweater and back up to her flaming face. He nodded. 'But tempting. I see you as a challenge.'

She opened her mouth to retort, but when she saw the look in his eyes, hungry, almost predatory, her anger began to turn to a distinct apprehension. She resented and detested him, but he gave off such an air of powerful masculinity that she felt suddenly helpless in his grasp.

In the silence of the room an almost palpable tension began to build up between them. They stood motionless, their eyes locked together, and Bianca had the odd sensation that they were the only two people in the universe at that moment.

She watched, frozen in place, as his head came slowly down towards her, his burning gaze never faltering, until finally, physically unable to move, she closed her eyes and felt his mouth settle firmly over hers. At the touch of his lips, an electric current shot through her, half pain, half pleasure, but totally undeniable.

The confident mouth was moving now, tugging gently at her lips, then opening slightly in a more demanding kiss. At the same time, he was pulling her towards him so that her slim body was pressed against his, and when his arms came around her back to hold her close, she drew in her breath sharply at the sudden contact with hard, masculine bone and muscle.

His large hands were travelling, up into her short dark hair, down her back, to her hips and back up to cup her face, but the firm pressure of his mobile mouth on hers never faltered.

Bianca was so stunned by this sudden assault on her senses that she couldn't think, couldn't move. Her head was whirling. The sweetness of his kiss, the feel of his warm strong hands on her face, the smell of his skin, were all so overwhelming to her that she could only stand there, helpless and pliable in his embrace.

Then, in a deft, practised movement, his hand glided lightly down over the front of her body, and before she knew what he was doing, the hand had reached up under her sweater and was firmly clasping her breast, covered only by a thin cotton shirt.

'And to think I thought you were a boy,' he murmured smoothly against her mouth as the hand moved to her other breast, moulding and stroking the hidden fullness with clever, experienced fingers.

At the sound of his voice, Bianca snapped back

into reality. She placed her hands firmly on his broad chest and with all her strength gave a mighty shove.

'No!' she cried, grey eyes blazing.

The push was so sudden and so obviously unexpected that Gerry teetered backward, almost losing his balance.

'What the hell?' he muttered, gazing at her in bewilderment, and reaching out for her again.

She took two hurried steps backward, out of his reach, and stood there hugging her arms tightly across her chest, glaring at him, red-faced and panting.

'Get out of my house,' she spat at him.

He took a step towards her, and she reached out and grabbed a pewter vase from the table beside her. 'Come one step closer, and I'll bash your head in,' she threatened, raising the heavy vase in the air.

She watched warily as the expression on the handsome face turned from puzzlement to anger and finally, seeing she meant what she said, to sullen resentment.

'Okay, okay,' he muttered. 'Put that damn thing down.'

'Not until you're out of here and the door is locked behind you.' Her voice was firm.

He stared at her for a long time, the battle raging within him clearly visible on his expressive features, until finally his wide mouth quirked up in amusement. He stood chuckling to himself for a moment, then, to her amazement, threw his dark head back and broke into laughter.

Bianca didn't know what to do. In her heart, all along, she was certain he wasn't dangerous. She felt a little foolish now brandishing the vase, especially since she knew she could never bring herself to hit him with it. With as much dignity as she could muster, she set the vase back down on the table, folded her arms in front of her and stood waiting for his hilarity to subside.

Finally, he quit laughing and held his hands up in the air. 'Truce,' he said with a grin. 'I surrender.'

'It's not funny,' she mumbled. 'You had no right to come barging in here and attack me like that.'

His heavy black, eyebrows shot up. 'Attack you! For God's sake, it was only a kiss. And,' he added dryly, 'I wasn't doing it alone.'

She reddened deeply. 'Well, pawing, then.' She gave him a defiant look.

He shrugged good-naturedly. 'Okay,' he agreed. 'Pawing, if that's what you want to call it. Didn't you like it? I've never had complaints before.'

Bianca's eyes widened. 'Why, you insufferable, conceited, egotistical . . .' she spluttered.

He frowned. 'I'm not sure I like your choice of words.'

'Well, isn't that too bad?' she drawled. 'Look, you may actually be the answer to every maiden's prayer for all I know, but as long as we're going to be neighbours, I want to make one thing absolutely clear.' She paused, groping for words.

He stood waiting politely, his thumbs hooked in the waistband of his jeans, a mock serious look on his face. 'Yes,' he prompted. 'Go on.'

She turned away, furious at his teasing tone. 'You know what I mean. I don't want any involvement.'

'Physical involvement?' he suggested softly.

She looked straight at him. '*Any* involvement. Period.'

'Why not?' He seemed serious. 'You're an attractive girl with all the right equipment in all the right places.' His dark eyes swept over her body. 'You enjoyed the kiss.'

'That's beside the point,' she retorted, flushing again. She lifted her chin. 'I'm a serious musician. I have a long way to go to become the kind of performer I want to be. I don't have time for—for—dalliance.'

He laughed again. 'Dalliance!' he repeated, spluttering. 'Where did you get a word like that?'

'You know what I mean,' she said evenly.

He stared at her for a long moment, then smiled crookedly at her. 'Sure,' he said. 'Of course I do. And I respect it. Really. I do. You're a professional. I could tell that from the way you played.'

The disarming smile caught at Bianca's heart for a second. What an attractive man, she thought, and knew that she would have to be on her guard against him, against her own weakness.

'Thank you,' she said primly.

He turned then and strode towards the back door. Watching him, Bianca thought she had never seen anyone move so gracefully. All his movements, gestures, mannerisms, expressions—everything about him, in fact—were perfect. Almost too perfect.

At the door, he turned and smiled briefly. 'We can be friends, though, can't we, Bianca? After all, we *are* neighbours.'

She nodded dumbly, but before she could reply, or voice her reservations, he was gone. She heard the sliding glass door swish shut behind him, the sound of his jaunty footsteps on the wooden verandah and stairs, and the room seemed suddenly empty, as though all the life had gone out of it.

Bianca walked slowly to the door and shot the bolt. Down below, on the beach, she could see Gerry's shadowy form walking back to the house next door. His shoulders were hunched over, his hands shoved into the pockets of his heavy jacket, his steps firm and unhurried.

She sighed and turned back to the quiet room. An unsettling experience, she thought, remembering his kiss, the way his mouth had felt on hers, the smooth hand on her breast, and the strong arms holding her close.

An unsettling *man*, she amended, as she turned out the lights and went slowly down the hall to her bedroom. A dangerous man. He was clever, she knew. He had handled the situation perfectly, with the practised skill of a man with absolute confidence in his ability to dominate a woman. He had played his roles to perfection, first the friendly next-door neighbour, then the gentle seducer, then the demanding lover, then the outraged male, the chagrined little boy, and finally the respectful, understanding friend.

Oh, he was good, all right, she thought, lying in the darkness and listening to the pounding surf through the open window. She tossed in the bed, wishing for the first time in her life that she'd had more experience with men. As a budding artist, she had been so sheltered from the realities of life, living like a nun in her single-minded dedication to music, her career.

What had gone wrong? Was it just the disturbing encounter with Gerry, or did it go deeper than that? She thought about her two sisters and wondered how they handled relations with men, but soon realised that there was no comparison. Norma was firmly entrenched in her singing career and Laura totally involved in her painting. She couldn't imagine either one of them allowing a man like Gerry to ruffle their composure in the slightest.

Was that the key? Was there some important connection between her response to Gerry tonight and her growing feeling of incompetence as an artist? But was it incompetence? Coming from a family of artists, Bianca knew that competence was not enough, that without the drive to excel, mere ability was a feeble support.

She lay there in bed staring at the ceiling. Skill could be learned, she thought, but drive had to come from within. In a sudden burst of clarity, she knew she had felt more alive in Gerry's arms than she ever had on the concert stage.

She smiled to herself as she recalled the devilishly attractive man's changes of mood. Oh, he was a scoundrel, all right, no doubt about it, and Bianca was certain he hadn't played all the cards in his deck as far as she was concerned.

What would be next? She tried to guess, but sleep overtook her before she got far. The last thought in her mind was that no matter what it was, she would be no match for him in any game he chose to play.

CHAPTER THREE

THE morning sunshine streaming in through the bedroom window seemed to bring with it a resolution of Bianca's confusion next morning. She sat up in bed and stretched widely, a new sense of purpose filling her mind.

After breakfast, she sat down at the telephone and dialled Tom Schiffren's number. She was confident now that she understood the strange impact Gerry had had on her last night. He had come along just when she was feeling shaky about her own career. Somehow, predator that he was, he must have sensed her vulnerability, and instinctively leaped into the gap, certain she would fall into his arms.

Think again, Gerry, she muttered to herself as she listened to the buzzing of the telephone in her ear. I'm a musician, not a plaything for a man like you.

'Hello.'

'Tom, it's Bianca.'

The low masculine voice warmed immediately. 'Bianca. I was hoping you'd call. How's it going?'

'Not bad. Listen, Tom, I won't keep you. I just wanted to ask if you were serious about coaching me.'

'Of course,' was the quick reply. 'I'm free on Tuesday and Thurday afternoons, if that suits your schedule.'

She laughed. 'I have no schedule. I'm on vacation, remember? Any time that's convenient for you. Do you want me to come to your studio at the university?'

'No. That won't be necessary. I need to get away from the amateur screechings around here anyway. Today is Tuesday. How about Thursday afternoon?'

'Sounds great. Can you come for lunch?'

'I'd love to. Around twelve, then?'

'Fine. See you then.'

As she replaced the receiver in its cradle, Bianca smiled to herself. So much for Gerry, she thought. That unsettling little scene last night was just what she'd needed to get her back on the track and show her what it was she really wanted. And what she definitely didn't want was an involvement with the arrogant, conceited playboy next door.

She walked to the sliding glass door leading on to the verandah and slid it open. A warm breeze blowing up from the blue sea fanned her short dark hair back from her face. The little black kitten she had adopted scooted past her, sniffed the air delicately, then gracefully stretched out on the warm wooden flooring in the sunshine.

'You've got the right idea, Midnight,' she murmured. 'Soak up the sun while it lasts.'

She turned back into the house and walked briskly down the hall to the bedroom. Dressing hurriedly in a pair of white shorts and a blue halter top, and slipping a pair of sandals on her bare feet, she went back out on to the sunny verandah to stretch out on the padded chaise next to Midnight.

After half an hour of facing the sun, she began to feel cooked and rolled over on her stomach to toast her back. She didn't want to overdo it and end up with a bad burn.

She closed her eyes and let her mind drift. It was good to have a sense of direction again, she thought. If Tom could help her two days a week and she practised hard in between, in a few months she'd be able to start performing again. Maybe a group at first, a quartet or small orchestra. The literature for chamber music was virtually endless, from the baroque style of Vivaldi and Pachelbel through all the romantics like Mendelssohn, Brahms, Beethoven, clear up to the modern dissonance of Shostakovich and Bartók. Every great composer wrote chamber music, it seemed, and there was something about the intimacy of playing with a small group that was far more satisfying than solo or symphony work.

She didn't realise she had drifted off to sleep until a gentle, sensuous stroking motion up and down her bare back suddenly jolted her awake. Disorientated for a moment, her eyes shot open and she lay motionless trying to collect her thoughts, to place in her mind the source of that pleasant sensation.

Then an alarm rang in her head, and she twisted around to see Gerry sitting beside her on the chaise, a tube of suntan cream in one hand, the other moving rhythmically along her rib cage, and a self-satisfied smirk on his good-looking face. His dark eyes were half shut, and if he'd been a cat he would have been purring.

'What do you think you're doing!' she cried, brushing his hand off her bare skin.

He looked at her. 'I'm administering first aid,' he said with a complacent grin. 'You were turning an interesting shade of red, and I didn't have the heart to wake you up.' The hand returned to her midriff.

Bianca firmly removed it and sat up to face him. 'You've got some nerve,' she breathed angrily.

'I was only trying to help,' he said in a hurt tone.

'I don't need your help. I thought I made that clear last night.'

She glared at him. He was sitting there as though he owned the world, dressed in dark bathing trunks and a white short-sleeved shirt unbuttoned down the front and revealing a wide expanse of smooth, beautifully tanned masculine chest.

Unbidden, the image flashed into Bianca's mind of the day she had seen him standing at the window of the house next door dressed only in his white undershorts. What had impressed her then at a distance was now seated dangerously close to her, and she didn't at all like the disturbing sensations his nearness created in her.

He was sitting in a relaxed posture, his knees apart, ankles crossed, the roaming hands resting now on his muscular, hair-roughened thighs. She glanced at the broad shoulders, the smooth chest, then down to the flat stomach where a light covering of dark hair disappeared into the waistband of the brief, low-slung shorts.

'Like what you see?' he asked pleasantly. Her eyes shot up to meet his, dark and faintly mocking. 'I'm enjoying the view myself.'

She flushed deeply as the hooded eyes travelled insolently down her body, knowing the flimsy halter top was scant covering for the high full breasts beneath. The white shorts also seemed to reveal far too much long, smooth, slightly reddened leg.

'Listen, Gerry,' she said, leaping to her feet and

standing over him. 'I don't know what game you're playing here, but whatever it is, I'm not interested.'

He looked up at her, a faint smile hovering about the sensuous mouth. What did it take, she wondered wildly, to discourage him? Then, slowly, he unwound his ankles and stood up facing her, not two inches of space separating them. She had to shift her position to look up at him, and somehow his height and all that muscle seemed to give him a superior advantage over her.

'I only came to invite you to a party,' he said at last.

She folded her arms in front of her and gave him a scornful look. 'Are you kidding? I've already heard one of your brawls, and believe me, I want no part of them.'

He gave her a long appraising look, the dark head tilted a little to one side, his expression inscrutable, probing, assessing.

'You know what your trouble is?' he said at last in a conversational tone. 'You're a snob.'

She stiffened at that and opened her mouth to protest, then realised he was only baiting her. What she wanted was to get rid of him, not defend herself against his accusations. What did she care what he thought?

She smiled coolly. 'Very well. I'm a snob. Then you certainly don't want me at your party. In fact, if I were you, I wouldn't want to bother with me at all. Now, goodbye. I have work to do.'

She turned away, pleased to see the uncertain frown gathering on his handsome face, and started walking purposefully towards the sliding glass door into the house.

'You really mean it, don't you?' came his stunned voice.

She turned to face him. 'Yes,' she said firmly. 'I really do.'

She was amazed, and a little touched, at his crestfallen expression. He was obviously a man quite unaccustomed to resistance to his blatant practised charm, and for a moment she had a brief glimpse of the real person underneath that monumental ego.

He scratched his dark head thoughtfully. 'I apologise,' he said at last, somewhat stiffly. 'I guess I'm so used to playing games I don't know how to handle the real thing when it comes along.'

She didn't know how to reply to that, and almost felt sorry for him. There was a long silence. Gerry continued to stare past her at some unseen object. She watched him carefully. He really was a terribly attractive man. The slight puzzled frown on his face made him seem so vulnerable, and the dark waving hair fell casually over his forehead, giving him a boyish look that she found less threatening, even quite appealing. She found her eyes straying dangerously down to that half-bare chest again, and made herself look away.

Finally he spoke. 'Well, Bianca, you don't want to play games with me, and you won't come to my party. What do you want?'

She sighed. 'Gerry, you have to understand. I don't dislike you, and I want to be a good neighbour, friends even, if it's possible. I really am serious about my music. I come from a family of dedicated artists of one kind or another. It's the way I was raised. It's in my genes. I don't belong in your world.'

'What is my world, Bianca?' he asked quietly. 'You don't really know anything about it.' He made an impatient gesture. 'I'm not sure I know what it is myself.' He gave her a long look. 'I won't bother you again.'

With that, he turned and left.

Bianca spent the next two days improving her suntan gradually and working harder than she ever had in her life. Tom had extremely high standards of musicianship, and she wanted to be ready for him when he came on Thursday. She dropped, exhausted, into bed each night, her fingers sore, shoulders aching, and her mind full of trills and arpeggios.

Although she found her mind wandering to thoughts of the strangely compelling man next door on several occasions, she was still able to dismiss him from her mind. He may be intensely appealing, she decided, whether in the macho image he liked to project or the vulnerable little boy she had seen last time they met, but in either role, she knew, he was dangerous to her. The time to cut him out of her life was now, before he could find a place in her heart. She knew instinctively that the kind of relationship he so clearly wanted from her would damage both her career and her own equilibruim. She couldn't afford to risk getting close to him.

By Thursday, when Tom Schiffren came to lunch, she had managed to avoid Gerry by the simple expedient of not going down to the beach. She knew he wouldn't be coming back to the house after their last encounter when she had dismissed him so firmly. Nor were there any signs of the party he had invited her to, and she wondered if he had just made up that invitation on the spur of the moment to get her attention.

When Tom came, her mind was so concentrated

on her work, she easily forgot all about her disturbing neighbour. It was good to see Tom, she thought as she greeted him, but she was surprised at how much older he looked than she remembered him. It had been at least four years since they'd met.

He was a slight fair man, only a few inches taller than Bianca's five feet seven, with a slim build and a thin, sensitive face. A dedicated musician, he was a fine violinist in his own right, as well as one of those rare teachers who sought not to impose his own will and musical interpretations on his students, but only to evoke what was best in them.

After lunch, she took out her violin, tuned it carefully at the piano and turned to him.

'Well, teacher, what do you want me to play?' she asked lightly. Her hands shook a little, and she realised she was more nervous than she would have thought possible.

'How about a few warm-up scales,' he suggested with an encouraging smile.

She returned his smile. He was sitting in an armchair near the piano, and she stood before him at the music stand, violin tucked under her chin, bow at the ready.

He listened attentively as Bianca went through several scales, major, minor and chromatic. His long tapering fingers drummed silently on his knees, keeping time, and his eyes were fastened on her flying fingers as they moved over the strings.

'Okay,' he said when she had finished. 'Now try a C major scale slowly, very, very slowly, drawing out each note, up to the highest treble octave you can reach comfortably.'

She nodded. Holding the violin firmly in place with her chin, she wiped her damp palms on the legs of her jeans and took up the bow again to start the difficult exercise, one that would test not only the steadiness of her touch, but the tone quality of each note.

When she had finished, Tom sat for a long time staring up at the ceiling, deep in thought. Bianca stood waiting for him to speak. Finally, he lifted his hands and made a nervous, impatient gesture in the air.

'You're rusty, Bianca,' he said severely at last.

She flushed. 'I know.' Her voice was low, almost inaudible.

He darted a quick glance at her red face. 'Your technique is all right, but something's missing. Play Bach's Air for G String for me now.'

Bianca cleared her throat and sought for the familiar music in her mind. Then she played the short, hauntingly beautiful melody with all the skill she could muster. When she was through, she waited again for him to speak.

First he frowned, deep in thought, then he nodded and stood up abruptly.

'Yes, the technique is fine, but you know as well as I do that anybody who's willing to practice hard can develop a good technique. What separates a fine violinist from a mere fiddler, however, is in here'—he pointed at his head—'and in here,' and he placed his hand over his heart.

He started pacing the room, moving in jerky nervous strides, his hands in the pockets of his tan trousers. Finally, he came back to stand before her. His expression was serious, almost pained.

'I don't want you to be just a fiddler, Bianca,' he said softly. 'There's more to you than that.'

'I wonder,' she murmured. She was crushed at his criticism, but knew in her heart that he was right, that the flaws he saw in her interpretation were the same ones she had already recognised in herself and which had led her to cancel the Boston concert in despair.

'Now, we're not going to have any self-pity,' Tom said in a firm voice. 'You've got the makings of a really top-notch musician, and you are not going to run away from it. I won't let you.'

Bianca was shocked at the urgency in his tone and stared at him, open-mouthed. He looked almost angry. Suddenly, out of the blue came the memory of the girlish crush she'd had on him so many years ago, and the thought occurred to her now that perhaps it hadn't been as one-sided as she'd imagined.

Looking at him now, the sensitive features, the smooth fair hair and expressive grey eyes, she wondered how old he was. There were fine lines on his forehead, deeper ones running from his nose to his thin mouth. Close to forty, by now, she guessed.

As though aware of the direction of her thoughts, he turned away from her and began pacing again. When he was across the whole length of the room from her, he turned around.

'Have you ever been in love, Bianca?'

Totally nonplussed, she could only stare. Then she thought, he really seemed to want an answer. She searched her mind and heart as honestly as she was able.

'No,' she said at last. 'Not really.'

She thought he flinched slightly at that, but if so, he covered it immediately with a slow smile of satisfaction.

'I didn't think so. You might be one of those artists who can't really create until they've suffered, and, believe me,' he added feelingly, 'an unhappy—or unrequited—love is the most excruciating pain known to man.'

She smiled. 'You say that as though you've had first-hand experience.'

He seemed to flinch again, but then chuckled gently. 'You don't get to be my age without a few hard knocks in that direction.' He became serious then, and began walking towards her. 'I mentioned two places, Bianca. Heart *and* head. We'll have to let nature take care of the heart aspect, but we can do something about the head.'

He went to the pile of music stacked on the piano and flipped through it. 'Here,' he said, pulling out a folder, 'here's a good example. Take this Brahms concerto.'

She went to his side and watched as he pointed out certain passages to her, concentrating, trying to grasp the point he was making.

'You must always ask yourself what the composer intended. Each passage makes a statement. Concentrate especially on the dynamics. Think about them. Use your intelligence. Why does Brahms mark this passage *piano*?' he asked, pointing. 'And the same passage a few bars later *fortissimo*? Why does he put an accent on this B flat, and not that one? Why is the tempo picked up so abruptly in this movement? Why is one arpeggio played *legato*, another *staccato*?' He looked at her. 'Do you understand what I'm saying?'

'I think I'm beginning to,' she said slowly. 'I've concentrated so hard on perfecting my technique, I guess I've never really thought through the composer's meaning.'

He smiled. 'That's only natural. Technique is

indispensable. It's got to be there before you can do anything else. It just isn't everything.'

'Yes,' she said breathlessly and looked at him with shining eyes. 'I see now what you mean.'

Their eyes met. They were standing so close now that their arms were touching. Suddenly, the room was very still, and for a brief moment, Bianca had the distinct impression that Tom was going to kiss her. Before she could make up her mind whether she wanted him to or not, however, he turned from her and set the music back on top of the pile.

'I'm going to give you some homework,' he said stiffly. 'Keep on practising an hour or two every day so your technique doesn't get rusty, but I want you to concentrate on thinking about the music. Let's focus on the Brahms. Get a good biography. Listen to his other music. Symphonies. Piano works. Get inside his head and heart. *Be* Brahms. *Think* Brahms. That's the way to go.'

By the time he left, Bianca's head was whirling. He had opened up a whole new approach to music. At last there was something she could *do*, and she was determined to give this new world of musical experience her best.

Later that evening, as she sat out on the verandah watching the sunset over the broad ocean, she thought about the odd moment that afternoon when she had been so sure Tom was going to kiss her, wanted to kiss her. What would her response have been if he had?

She finally had to admit she didn't know. She was fond of Tom. At one time she'd been more than fond of him. She thought, too, about his question whether she had ever been in love, and it occurred to her with a sudden blaze of insight that she could have Tom now if she wanted him. Did she want him? Did she want any man?

She wondered about her sisters, both of them so much older than she. She knew nothing about their personal lives. Laura had lived in Malibu alone for years. Norma spent her life travelling the opera circuit. Both were fine artists. Had they had love affairs?

Then, out of the blue, she thought about Gerry, comparing him in her mind to Tom. Two men could hardly be more different. She and Tom had so much in common, and she'd known him forever. She felt so comfortable with him, and still found him attractive. Gerry, on the other hand, was an unknown quantity, totally outside her experience, her world. She found him profoundly disturbing, even dangerous.

The sun had set, filling the western sky with bright streaky patterns of orange and gold. The first stars began to appear as the sky darkened, and she sat quietly, listening to the gulls screeching at each other.

As soon as the colour was gone from the sky, she felt a chill on her bare shoulders and shivered a little, hugging her arms closely. Better go in, she thought, and as she slowly rose to her feet, the thought came to her that if it was an unhappy love affair she needed to perfect her music, Gerry would be an ideal candidate. There was no way an affair with him could possibly end except with her own suffering.

She picked up the black kitten from the chaise and went inside. As she slid the glass door shut behind her and bolted it securely, she decided firmly that nothing—not even her music—was worth the risk of that kind of pain. It wasn't even a risk, she thought as she set Midnight down on the kitchen floor. It was a certainty, and she closed her mind against it.

Late Saturday night, just two days after Tom's visit, Bianca was once again awakened out of a sound sleep by the blast of raucous music coming from the house next door. She'd been leaving her bedroom window open at night now that the evenings were warmer, and this time the awful din was even worse then last.

She sat bolt upright in bed, recognised the source of the wild shrieks and pounding beat, then flopped back on her pillow. Honestly, she thought in disgust, you'd think he'd have more consideration for his poor neighbours.

She turned on her stomach and pulled the covers up over her head, but the noise hardly abated. She sat up again, glanced at the clock on the nightstand beside the bed and groaned. Three o'clock in the morning. There ought to be a law. Maybe there was, and for one grim moment, she considered calling the police. It would serve him right.

With a sigh, she slipped out of bed, threw a thin robe on over her cotton nightgown and started to the kitchen to make a cup of cocoa. There was no point in trying to sleep. On her way out of the bedroom she slammed the window shut. It helped a little.

She flipped on the kitchen light and got out the milk and cocoa. As she stood at the stove warming it, she yawned deeply. Glancing out the window as she stirred, she could see the bright full moon shining in the dark cloudless sky. She smiled to herself. After all, she thought, I don't have to get up early. What difference does it make if I lose a little sleep?

When the cocoa was heated, she poured some into a mug and went out on the verandah to get a better look at the beautiful night sky. A gentle breeze wafted over her. It was quite warm.

There was a sudden blissful lull in the loud music coming from next door. Bianca moved over to the railing of the verandah and leaned slightly over the edge to get a better look. Once again, the house was blazing with light, and she could hear sounds of laughter, people calling to each other, a woman's high shriek. It sounded as though they were having a good time, but it wasn't her idea of fun.

She turned her gaze back to the sea, scanning the darkness, enjoying the sudden peace and quiet. Gradually, she managed to tune out the voices from the party, and she began to experience the delicious sensation that she was all alone in this starlit universe.

Then a sudden movement on the beach below caught her eye. Curious, and a little apprehensive, she glanced down to see a large dark shape in the shadows, out of the light still streaming through the kitchen window.

'Is that you, Juliet?' came a deep, masculine voice.

She blinked, startled, trying to adjust her eyes. Then she realised it was Gerry speaking and had to smile.

'What are you doing down there, you fool?' she called softly.

'Taking a walk. Enjoying the view.'

There was a teasing, seductive quality to his voice, and it dawned on her that although she could barely make out his shape, she herself was well-illuminated by the lights from inside. She pulled her robe tighter around her, propped her elbows on the railing and leaned over a little farther.

'You mean you've left your own party?' she mocked. 'How rude.'

'It's not my party,' he retorted.

Her eyes were accustomed to the darkness now, and she could see him more clearly. He was standing just below the verandah, his hands in the pockets of his jeans, staring up at her. She couldn't make out the expression on his face in the dimness, but she could well imagine the slow, knowing smile on that beautiful, sensuous mouth.

'What do you mean it's not your party?' she asked tartly. 'You invited me, didn't you?'

She saw him lift his broad shoulders in a slight shrug. 'Well, when you said you wouldn't come, I cancelled it, but they came anyway.'

She giggled a little. 'You're crazy, you know that?'

'I do, indeed, Juliet.' He paused. 'Come on down.'

'I can't. I'm not dressed.'

'Good,' was the immediate reply.

She laughed shortly. 'I'm not that big a fool.'

'I'll come up, then.'

'No you won't,' she replied firmly.

There was another pause. 'What are you drinking?'

'Cocoa.'

'Gee, that sure sounds good.' There was a wistful note in his voice.

'It seems to me that there's plenty of liquid refreshment at your place—among other things,' she remarked dryly. She remembered Laura's comments about the Southern Californian acidheads, and had visions of a marijuana and cocaine orgy.

He chuckled deep in his throat. 'It's not that kind of party.' There was a short silence. Then, 'I'd sure like a cup of cocoa,' he remarked in a pathetic tone.

'Well, you're not getting one,' she said firmly.

'Not even if I promise to behave?' His voice was so low she could barely hear him.

'I don't trust you,' she said, but she knew she was wavering.

The trouble was, she thought, she liked him. He was dangerous, she knew, but there was an insouciant charm about him that she found very appealing in spite of his arrant egotism. He was probably perfectly harmless. She was wide awake and wouldn't mind a little company. Still, there definitely was an element of danger in him. She would have to be on her guard against that.

While she was still debating within herself whether to let him come up, she heard a bounding tread on the wooden stairs and the next thing she knew he was walking towards her.

She could see him quite clearly now that he was in the light, and she stared at him, wide-eyed, as he approached her slowly. My goodness, he's a handsome man, she thought. The shadowy light sharpened the angles of his face and caught the gleam in the dark eyes. His black hair was tousled, as usual, falling over his forehead, curling around his ears, and he was wearing a white shirt, open at the neck.

'You've got some nerve,' she remarked coolly. He stood before her now, grinning down at her. 'I don't remember inviting you up here.'

He folded his tanned muscular arms in front of him and rested his lean hips back against the railing. The eyes were hooded now, the grin lazy, appraising, as he gazed at her.

'You can trust me,' he said softly. 'All I want is a cup of cocoa. Promise.'

'What about your guests?' She gestured to the house next door.

'They won't even know I'm gone,' he said in a positive tone.

'Why are you gone?' she asked, suddenly curious.

He shrugged. 'I don't know. It's their party. They invited themselves.'

'Don't you like that kind of party?'

The grin widened. 'I'm trying to wean myself away from them.' She gave him a dubious look. 'I really am,' he said in a more serious tone. 'It's just not that easy to break old ties.'

She thought that over for a moment, then smiled at him, deciding to take him at his word. 'Do you really want a cup of cocoa?'

He nodded solemnly. 'I really do.'

'You're making fun of me again!'

He pushed himself away from the railing in a lithe, graceful motion and reached out a hand to her cheek, brushing it lightly with his fingertips. 'No, I'm not, Bianca. It's just my way. Now, will you please get me a cup of cocoa?'

Without a word she turned from him and went inside. That touch had shaken her, and she didn't want him to see it. As she got down another mug from the cupboard, she was dismayed to see how her hand trembled. She set the mug down on the counter and turned the burner on under the pot of cocoa. While she waited for it to heat, she tried to think coherently about what was happening to her.

No man had ever had quite the disturbing effect on her as Gerry seemed to create, just by his mere presence. The impact of his compelling good looks and assured manner confused her, made her feel gauche and inexperienced. Well, she thought, switching off the burner and pouring cocoa into the mug, wasn't she gauche and inexperienced?

That had never seemed to matter before. Up until now, except for that brief crush on Tom Schiffren, the whole area of relations between the sexes had been a closed book to her. She didn't like the way Gerry made her feel when he touched her, or even looked at her in that certain confident way he had, but still she found it definitely pleasant to be viewed as desirable by such an attractive man.

As she walked slowly back out to the verandah, steadier now after those few moments alone, she had to laugh at herself. What had he done, after all? A kiss, a touch, a look. They meant nothing. She had been too sheltered. Why not just enjoy his company? It was music that filled her life. She could handle Gerry. He wasn't going to attack her, or rape her, for heaven's sake. She'd been blowing the whole thing out of all proportion.

She stepped lightly through the doorway on to the verandah, feeling more confident now. He was standing at the far edge, his back to her, leaning over, his arms braced along the railing. She caught her breath and stopped short when she saw the broad back, the way the muscles strained against the thin cloth of his white shirt. The thick dark hair grew low on the nape of his neck so that it touched the collar, and she couldn't help wondering how it would feel in her fingers.

For a moment, her resolution faltered, and she had a strong urge to run back inside, slam the door shut and bolt it against him. Then he straightened up, stretched a little and turned around. When he saw her standing there, he smiled broadly.

'Ah,' he said, 'my cocoa.'

She walked towards him, the mug in her outstretched hand, and returned a weak smile of her own. With each step she took, she had the feeling that she was moving closer to some point of no return, and the thought crossed her mind that that point could mean either an exciting adventure or her own doom.

CHAPTER FOUR

'I've been listening to you practice.' He had settled himself comfortably on the padded chaise and was looking up at her over the mug of cocoa. 'I'm impressed.'

She held her own mug in both hands to keep it steady. 'I wish my teacher felt the same,' she remarked with a nervous laugh.

'Your teacher? Is that the artistic type who was over here the other day? Short, skinny guy?'

'Yes, Tom Schiffren. He's a real slave driver.' Short and skinny? Compared to Gerry, he probably was, she thought.

'He looked like a real wimp to me.'

She opened her mouth to make a sharp retort in Tom's defence, then realised he was merely baiting her. 'Looks can be deceiving,' she said at last.

He raised an eyebrow at that and gave her a thoughtful look. 'Are you trying to tell me something?'

'What do you mean? I don't understand.'

'Okay, I'll spell it out. Are you sleeping with him?'

She choked on a swallow of cocoa and almost dropped her mug. 'With Tom?' she gasped. Then a slow flush of anger began to flow through her. 'You've got a lot of brass asking me a question like that. It's none of your business. How would you like it if I asked you who you were sleeping with?'

'Are you?'

She gave him a blank look. 'Am I what?'

'Asking me who I'm sleeping with.'

'No, of course not. I don't care who you're sleeping with.'

'Don't you?'

'Of course not.'

'I'm crushed.' He eyed her carefully. 'I'll tell you anyway. I'm not sleeping with anyone. Now, are you happy?'

She could only stare. How had this conversation started in the first place? she wondered. Now he'd twisted it around so that he was responding to a demand she'd never made. Finally, she decided the only way to handle the awkward situation was to laugh at him, treat his bantering, suggestive innuendo as a joke.

'You're impossible,' she said at last with a smile. 'You know that?'

He grinned. 'You have a wonderful smile. It goes well with that messy mop of hair.'

'You're one to talk!' she retorted, eyeing his own dark head meaningfully.

He laughed. 'Come and sit down,' he said, patting the narrow space on the chaise beside him. 'You make me nervous standing there.'

Bianca couldn't imagine him nervous under any conceivable circumstances, and she certainly had no intention of sitting down on that chaise. His large body sprawled gracefully over most of the surface of the pad, leaving barely enough room for even her slim form.

She set her mug down on the round metal table and turned to reach for one of the folding aluminum chairs stacked up against the house, when she felt a firm grip on her arm pulling her off balance. Before she could regain her equilibrium, she found herself seated beside him on that narrow strip of padding. She could feel the warmth and hardness of his body through her nightgown and robe, and immediately started to jump to her feet. His grip on her arm was firm, however, and she couldn't move.

'Relax, Bianca,' he said softly. 'I won't hurt you. I'm just a very affectionate guy. I like you, so I want to feel you close to me. That's all.'

As if to prove his point, he released her arm and moved an inch or so away from her so that they weren't pressed quite so closely together. He locked his arms behind his head and rested back on them.

Bianca wasn't sure what to do. She was tempted to get up and walk inside the house and leave him out there alone. She was also tempted to stay right where she was. She looked at him. He seemed harmless.

'You're incorrigible,' she said at last.

'I know.' There was a note of satisfaction in his voice.

'Also arrogant, pushy, conceited, irresponsible . . .'

'Hey, hold on. You're going to hurt my feelings in a minute.'

'I honestly don't think that's possible,' she said, dead serious.

He gave her an odd look. 'Oh, it's possible, Bianca,' he said softly. Then, 'Look, I'm not looking for an involvement. God knows I've had enough of those. I just like you. You're different. I admire your dedication to music, your professionalism. We're going to be neighbours for a while. Why can't we be friends?'

He seemed quite serious, for a change, she

thought, watching him. The mocking smile and knowing look were gone. And, oh, Lord, she thought irrationally, he's even more attractive when he's not kidding around. Well, he only wanted to be friends. She *did* like him, and they *were* neighbours.

'All right,' she said at last. 'Friends.'

'Shake,' he said and extended a hand.

She took it with a smile, and the next thing she knew she was pressed up against him, his arms around her, his mouth covering hers in a hard, demanding kiss. Caught totally off-guard, Bianca found herself responding to the pressure of the firm lips in spite of herself. Her mouth softened under his, and she quite enjoyed the way his large hands were stroking up and down her back.

Then she felt the tip of his tongue against her lips, and she stiffened. Gauche and inexperienced she may be, she thought wildly, but she knew that wasn't the way 'friends' kissed each other. Then, when she felt experienced fingers begin to slide tantalisingly from her back, over her fragile ribcage to settle on one firm, high breast, she gasped and wrenched her head back. Glaring at him, she struggled vainly to twist herself out of that iron grip.

'You lied to me!' she accused furiously.

'Now what makes you say a thing like that?' He bent his head to nuzzle along her jawline and up to her ear. The hand moved sensuously to explore her other breast. 'I told you I was a very affectionate person.'

'Well, I'm not,' she choked out. 'Now, let go of me.' The touch of his hand on her breast had left a path that felt like liquid fire in her bloodstream, delicious, wonderful, but shattering.

'Okay,' he said at last with a sigh. His hands and mouth left her, and he settled back on the chaise. 'Have it your way.' He smiled. 'It's just that you're very tempting sitting there in your robe, so cool, so distant. I can't resist trying to get a reaction from you.'

Which he had, she thought, flushing deeply. She jumped to her feet, still trembling. She was badly shaken. She'd never been kissed or touched like that before, hardly ever been kissed at all except for giggling juvenile experiments when she was in school. All of the men she knew were more interested in music than romance.

She finally managed to get herself under control. Somehow she would have to make Gerry understand. She looked down at him.

'Gerry,' she said slowly, 'if we're going to be friends you've got to quit making these sneak attacks on me.'

'You didn't like it?' He seemed to be sincerely interested.

The trouble was, she had liked it too well, but she wasn't going to tell him that. 'That's beside the point,' she went on. 'I might learn to like heroin, but that doesn't mean it's good for me.' She paused. 'You have to understand, Gerry,' she went on in a low voice. 'My life . . . my family . . . the way I've lived.' She struggled to find the right words. 'Well, I've lived almost like a nun. It's the same with my brothers and sisters . . . We just haven't lived normal lives.' A wistful note crept into her voice. She shrugged helplessly and tried to smile. 'I'm afraid your idea of friendship isn't exactly the same as mine.'

He stood up now and gazed down at her. 'No. That's obvious. I apologise.' He frowned, then lifted his head and looked away from her. 'I come from a pretty free-and-easy lifestyle,' he said evenly. 'As I said earlier, I'm trying to wean myself away from it. I think maybe you could help me. I admire you very much.' He shoved his hands in the pockets of his jeans and hunched his shoulders. 'I'm trying . . .' He broke off, glanced down at her, then looked away again. 'I'm trying to be a more serious person.'

Bianca was touched, but still wary. Was his sudden humility just another role he was acting? She didn't trust him an inch. What game was he playing this time? What was he trying to tell her? She waited.

Finally he took a deep breath and expelled it noisily. He turned to look down at her again.

'I've written a book,' he announced at last. 'A novel. And it will be published soon. I'm working on the final revisions now.'

'Why, Gerry, that's wonderful. I'm impressed.'

He waved a hand in the air and frowned. 'Yes, it is wonderful in a way, but I'm finding that in order to keep writing I have to change, break old ties, give up the crazy life.'

She eyed him warily. He seemed sincere, but how could you tell with a person like Gerry? She knew nothing about him. They had no common ground for understanding, no shared past. He obviously came from an entirely different background from hers, and although she couldn't help liking him, she didn't trust him for a minute.

'What did you do before?' she asked. 'Before you started writing?'

He gave her a long searching look. 'This and that,' he said at last. 'A little acting, a little tending bar, a little of everything.'

She opened her mouth. 'I . . .' she began.

Then a shout came up from the beach, a high feminine voice calling out in the darkness. 'Gerry! Where are you, Gerry?' Silence. Then, 'I know you're out here somewhere. Come on back to the party.'

'Oh, hell,' he muttered. He gave Bianca a ong look, smiled a crooked rueful smile, then leaned over the verandah. 'Be right down, Flicka.' He turned back to Bianca. 'Gotta go now. If I don't, she'll come up here. See you. Thanks for the cocoa.'

She watched as he strolled nonchalantly away from her across the verandah, his movements confident and hurried. He started down the stairs, and in a moment disappeared from view. He never once looked back.

'Where have you been?' she heard the girl's voice cry. 'I've been looking all over for you. Everyone's leaving.'

Bianca heard the low rumble of his reply, then stood and watched as they emerged from the shadows into the light from the house. They were walking slowly towards the house next door, the tall broad-shouldered man and a shorter girl with long blonde hair that flowed silkily down to the waistband of her jeans. His arm was draped loosely around her shoulders, while hers clutched his waist, so close together that they cast only a single shadow.

A very affectionate guy, Bianca thought to herself dryly. Isn't that what he'd said? She could still taste his kiss on her lips, practised, experienced—and totally meaningless.

She went inside, turned out the lights, and went back to bed. It was quiet now that the party was over. She could get some sleep. Lying in the darkness, she thought of Gerry and couldn't help wondering what he and Flicka were doing at that moment. She'd said that everyone else was leaving. Did that mean she was spending the night with him? He'd said he wasn't sleeping with anyone. Was that another lie?

'Oh, come on, Bianca,' she muttered aloud. What difference did it make? She smiled at her own question. She could still feel the touch of his mouth, his magic hands. She couldn't help liking him, responding to him, but she was glad she'd made it clear to him, and to herself, that she meant it to stop right there.

Early the next morning, when Bianca slid open the door to the patio to let the crying Midnight out, she saw the girl with the long blonde hair again. Dressed in a ragged pair of cut-off jeans and a sleeveless sweatshirt, she was standing at the edge of the surf, the gentle morning tide lapping at her bare feet.

When Bianca opened the door the girl glanced up at the verandah, shielding her eyes from the bright morning sun. They stared at each other for several moments. Bianca had already showered and dressed and had on a pair of white shorts and a halter top. Her mop of curly dark hair shone in the sunshine, and her skin had turned a warm toasty brown by now.

Finally, the blonde girl started walking slowly towards the house. Her long straight hair was like cornsilk, and as she turned she brushed it casually back with a graceful flip of one hand.

Bianca stared at her, wondering as she approached just who she was and what her relationship with Gerry could be. From the way they had walked away last night with their arms around each other, she doubted it was a casual one. But, then, she thought grimly, he was a very affectionate guy.

The girl was smiling up at her now, standing just below the verandah, her hand still shielding her eyes. She was very lovely, Bianca thought. No wonder the amorous Gerry was so fond of her. She must have stayed the night. Another lie, Bianca thought bitterly. He'd said he wasn't sleeping with anyone.

'Hi,' the girl called up to her. 'I've been wanting to meet you.'

Bianca walked slowly to the railing and leaned over slightly. She didn't know what to say, but the girl's grin was infectious, open and friendly, and she smiled back at her. The girl moved closer, into the shadow of the verandah, and removed her hand from her eyes.

'I'm Flicka, Miss Jameson,' she announced. 'I've been trying to get up the nerve to come over and introduce myself ever since Gerry moved in.'

'Really?' Bianca replied weakly. Why would this girl want to meet her? Surely she didn't see her as a rival for the magnetic Gerry's affections? And how did she know her name?

'Yes,' Flicka went on more confidently. 'I'm an artist, too, you see,' she continued in a rush, her voice low and earnest. She was frowning, as though searching for the right words.

Bianca was puzzled. Why was the girl so nervous? And what kind of artist was she? And what in the world did it have to do with her?

'Oh,' she said lamely. 'You mean you're a musician? What's your instrument?'

'No, not that kind of artist. I'm a painter. At least, I'm trying to be. I'm enrolled at the Westwood Academy of Fine Arts. I want to paint portraits, too. I admire your work so much, Miss Jameson, and I was hoping you might take a look . . .'

'Hold on,' Bianca exclaimed with a laugh. 'You've got the wrong Jameson. I'm Bianca. You want my sister, Laura.'

'You're not Laura Jameson?' The girl was clearly puzzled. 'I thought this was her house.'

'Laura is my sister,' Bianca repeated. 'This is her house. She's in England for a year, and I'm just staying here.'

'Oh, dear, what a disappointment.'

Bianca had to smile. 'Sorry,' she said lightly. 'I can't even draw a straight line.'

The girl gave her a quick apologetic look. 'That was terribly rude of me to say that. I'm sorry.' She sighed deeply. 'It's just that I've been cranking myself up to come over here for weeks, and now . . .' She spread her hands helplessly.

Just then, Bianca caught out of the corner of her eye a tall male figure striding towards the house. It was Gerry. He was wearing a skimpy pair of dark bathing trunks and nothing else. Bianca felt a slow flush wash over her as she watched that confident walk and the powerful muscles playing under all that tanned masculine flesh. As he came closer, she could see that he was frowning.

Quickly, she looked away. It wasn't her fault if his little blonde playmate chose to come over and introduce herself. And why had he let Flicka believe she was Laura? If the girl had been plotting ways to approach her, surely the subject had been discussed between them.

'Flicka,' came Gerry's curt voice, 'I thought I told you . . .'

'I know what you told me, Gerry,' Flicka cut in. 'But, as you can see, I did it anyway.' She looked up at Bianca. 'He's been warning me about coming over here bothering you. That's why I did it while he was still asleep.'

Bianca squirmed uncomfortably. She didn't want to hear the details of their relationship. She wished they'd both just leave. She glanced at Gerry. He was standing a few feet away from the blonde girl, his large hands balled up into fists, resting lightly on his slim hips, his arms akimbo.

He did indeed look as though he'd just got up, she thought. His dark eyes seemed even more heavy-lidded than usual, and the wavy black hair, brilliant in the sunshine, even more disarranged. Still, Bianca thought that outside of paintings and statues, she had never seen such a beautiful man. He was simply splendid standing there practically naked, the long muscular legs darkened with coarse black hair, the broad bare shoulders and powerful chest gleaming.

He squinted up at her. 'You're up early for keeping such late hours.' He smiled.

'So are you,' she retorted severely. She was annoyed at him for lying to her about his love life. Not that it mattered to her in the least, she assured herself, but no one likes to be lied to.

'Well, you can blame Flicka for that,' he said. He darted a glance of annoyance at the blonde girl, who only grinned at him. 'She makes so much noise in the morning.' He glared at her. 'She also leaves long blonde hairs in the bathroom sink, doesn't pick up after herself, disturbs me when I'm trying to work, invites all *her* noisy friends to *my* house, and generally manages to make an unholy pest of herself.'

Bianca could hardly believe her ears. What was going on here? A lovers' quarrel of some kind? It didn't sound like one, unless it was Hollywood-style. Gerry seemed to be seriously annoyed, and she had the feeling his anger stemmed from the fact that the lovely Flicka had come over to introduce herself against his wishes. It appeared that even the insouciant Gerry hated to be caught out in a lie, and, true to masculine form, managed to turn his own guilt into anger at the person who had revealed his deception. The poor girl, Bianca thought, and gave her a look of sympathy.

Flicka, however, didn't seem to be upset in the least at Gerry's caustic tone and accusations. In fact, she was grinning from ear to ear, even though he was still glowering at her.

'Who cares what you think?' she retorted defiantly. 'I'm leaving today anyway.' She glanced up at the open-mouthed Bianca. 'I'm glad I got to meet you, anyway, Bianca, even if you aren't Laura Jameson. I'm sure we'll see each other again.' With that, she flounced past Gerry, gave him a hard shove that almost knocked him off balance, and said in a loud voice, 'Pooh to you, brother, dear.'

'Why you . . .' he muttered angrily. He reached out to smack her bottom, but she darted out of his reach and ran up the beach, laughing gaily. For a moment, it looked as though he was going after her, but he stayed put and looked up at Bianca.

Brother! He was Flicka's brother. Bianca was caught totally off-guard. He hadn't lied. A warm feeling of relief ran through her. She met his dark eyes and watched as a half smile gradually replaced the thunderous frown on his face. He shook his head slowly from side to side.

'That kid,' he muttered. 'What a pest! She's been my cross since the day she was born.'

'Poor Gerry,' Bianca mocked. 'How you suffer. I really feel sorry for you.'

'Enough for you to give me a cup of coffee?' he rejoined in a flash.

Bianca sighed. 'Oh, all right. Come on up.'

She went inside to get the coffee and mugs, and when she returned, he was seated comfortably on the chaise, his long legs apart, elbows resting on his knees. She stopped short at the doorway. It was one thing to see all that bare masculine flesh down on the beach, but quite another to view it at such close quarters. His body unnerved her, and her legs weren't quite steady as she moved slowly out on to the verandah and set the tray down on the round metal table.

'Aren't you afraid you'll get burned without a shirt on?' she mumbled as she poured. She was trying hard not to look at him, but he was so close it was unavoidable. She concentrated on his face.

He raised his eyebrows and twisted his head around to examine his shoulders. 'No. I've got enough tan by now. Take a look. Don't you think so?' He turned his upper body slightly and presented a clear view of his broad back.

She gave it a brief glance. 'I suppose you're right,' she murmured. She unfolded an aluminum chair and sat across the table from him.

'Mmm, this is good,' he said, taking a long swallow of the fresh, fragrant coffee. He settled back on the chaise and closed his eyes.

They sat in companionable silence for several

minutes, drinking coffee, soaking up the warmth of the sun, listening to the sound of the surf and the gulls crying to each other. Bianca felt totally relaxed and happy. She leaned her head back and closed her eyes, at peace with the world.

It was so pleasant to be here, she thought, and for the first time since she met him, she felt really comfortable with him. In spite of his scanty attire—which was normal for the beach anyway—he hadn't come on to her in any remotely provocative way. Maybe he'd got her message and they could be friends after all.

After a moment or two, she had a sudden feeling she was being watched. She opened her eyes to find him gazing at her thoughtfully.

'So, Bianca,' he said lazily, 'what are your plans?'

'Plans?'

'Sure. Plans. What are you going to do with yourself, your music?'

She frowned. 'I'm not sure.' She sat up and poured more coffee for them both. 'I came here to get away from music for a while, but I'm finding it impossible to resist.'

'Why did you want to do that?' A look of amazement crossed his face. 'I'm no expert, but you sound damn good to me. Too good to give it up.'

She sighed and looked away. 'I don't know if I'll ever be as good as I want to be. Or as good as my family wants me to be.'

'Tell me about your family.'

'Oh, they're wonderful,' she replied, brightening. She went on to recount all the accomplishments of her talented brothers and sisters, eagerly going into the details of Norma's opera career, Laura's painting success and the wonderful musical gifts of her father and two brothers.

When she had finished, Gerry was silent for a long time, gazing at her. Finally, he spoke. 'That's quite a formidable bunch of talent to live up to.'

'Yes, it is,' she said. The smile left her face. 'Too formidable, I sometimes think.'

He shrugged and set his cup down. 'When I first decided to try my hand at writing,' he said in a low serious tone, 'everyone said I was crazy. I was doing okay—well, more than okay—at what I was doing, but it wasn't what I really wanted.' He gave her a long look. 'Do what *you* want to do, Bianca. Don't spend your life trying to live up to your family's expectations. Make your plans based on your own dreams, not someone else's. It's the only way.'

She was touched at his concern, and had a sudden impulse to reach across the table and touch the large strong brown hand resting there. She didn't do it, though. What good did it do to warn him off if she were going to start touching him like that? Instead, she smiled.

'You're right, of course, and I've just about arrived at that conclusion myself. The music is in there somewhere. I know now that it's too much a part of me to give it up completely.' She straightened up in her chair. 'Actually, right now my major problem is financial. It costs me hardly anything to live here in Laura's house, but it does cost something, and I'm almost broke.'

'What will you do? I can give you some money if you need it.'

She reddened. 'Oh, no, Gerry, I wasn't . . . No. I shouldn't have said that. Besides, you're a struggling artist yourself.' He opened his mouth to speak, but she rushed on, embarrassed. 'I can always give lessons, or find a job playing in a group. I'm going to call Tom today to see if he knows of anything.'

'Tom,' he repeated. 'Your teacher, right?' She nodded. He set his mug down on the table and gave her a challenging look. 'The wimp.'

Bianca refused to let him bait her. She smiled tightly. 'As I said, looks can be deceiving. Tom is an old friend, a fine teacher, and a wonderful man.' She batted her eyes provocatively. 'Actually, I had a terrific thing about him a few years ago.'

'Don't do that,' he snapped, glaring at her.

Her eyes widened. 'Do what?'

'Come on to me like that.' His voice was grim with a distinctly threatening undertone. 'You don't realise what you do to a man, sitting there in that skimpy outfit, fluttering those long eyelashes.'

'You're one to talk,' she defended herself hotly. 'You're practically . . .' She stopped, appalled at the direction the conversation was taking.

'Practically naked?' he supplied for her pleasantly, glancing down at his bare chest. Then he looked at her. 'But I'm not as pretty as you are.' He cocked his head to one side and his dark eyes swept over her in a swift, inclusive appraisal. 'I don't think you know what a seductive baggage you are, with those fragile bones and wild mop of hair.' He grinned. 'A little on the thin side, but filled out quite nicely in all the right places.'

'Gerry,' she warned, flushing hotly under his penetrating gaze. No one had ever spoken to her like that before in her life. She didn't know how to handle it. On the one hand, his approval of her physical attributes pleased her, but, knowing him and his 'affectionate' nature, she was determined to stay off such dangerous ground. A man like

Gerry would chop her in little pieces and have her for breakfast if she allowed him to go past the boundaries she had so carefully erected.

'And your face,' he went on dreamily, ignoring her protest. 'Not exactly beautiful, but very, very interesting. Intense, intelligent, shows a lot of character.'

'Gerry,' she said again. 'Stop that right now.'

He laughed. 'Sorry, Bianca. The temptation to tease you is irresistible.' He rose slowly to his feet, stretched widely and flexed his shoulders forward so that his long arms were held straight out in front of him rigidly.

The abrupt motion startled her, caught her off-guard, and she watched, mesmerised, as the dark bathing trunks slipped down lower on his narrow hips under the tautened stomach muscles.

Then, recovering herself, she gave him a cool look. 'I'm impressed with your body,' she remarked dryly, 'but you're still wasting your time.'

For a brief moment, a look of real pain flashed in the dark eyes. He hitched up his trunks and folded his arms across his chest. 'You're a hard woman, you know that, Bianca?' He grinned. 'But I like you anyway. Thanks for the coffee. I'd better get to work.' He turned to go.

'Gerry,' she called after him when he had reached the top of the stairs. He turned back. 'Why didn't you want Flicka to come over here?'

He shrugged, then cocked his head to one side in that typical gesture of his. A slow smile formed on his mobile mouth. 'I don't know. Like I said before, you're different, kind of special. I guess I just didn't want to share you with anyone. Dumb, isn't it?' With a little wave he took off down the stairs.

Watching him striding up the beach, Bianca had to smile. She couldn't stay angry with him for long. He was too good-natured, too sure of himself and his appeal. She heard him whistle shrilly and saw Barney come bounding towards him, barking wildly and dancing in the sandy beach. Then, in one graceful fluid motion, Gerry dived headlong into the surf, the ecstatic dog right behind him.

Later that afternoon Bianca made up her mind she had better call Tom to see if he knew of any playing jobs. Her financial situation wasn't critical, but she'd feel more secure with some money coming in.

As she dialled his number, she thought about her playing. With her recent intensive practice, she felt more confident, but she had just about decided that she didn't really want to pursue a solo career. Music would always be an important part of her life, but she was beginning to seriously doubt that she had the drive and dedication it took to become a concert artist. She heard Tom's voice on the line.

'This is Professor Schiffren.'

'My, I'm impressed,' Bianca said lightly.

His voice warmed immediately. 'Bianca? It's good to hear from you. The damn phone has been ringing off the hook with budding musicians ever since I started here.'

'That bad?'

He groaned. 'You have no idea. I think my university career is going to be quite brief. I prefer coaching serious students. All these kids seem to want is a free ticket to quick success. They're far more interested in my connections than my musical expertise.'

'Oh, Tom, that's too bad.'

'Well, enough of that. How about you? Are you practising hard? Doing your homework?'

'Yes,' she replied truthfully. 'I'm soaking myself in Brahms. Laura has a wonderful record collection, and I'm going to the library this afternoon to look for a biography.'

'Good girl.' He laughed shortly. 'I wish my other students were as obedient and pliable.'

'Tom, the reason I called . . .' She hesitated. 'I was just wondering,' she plunged on, 'if you knew of any playing jobs around that I could audition for.'

There was a short silence. 'I'm thinking,' he said at last. 'We do get calls here occasionally for musicians to fill in. What did you have in mind?'

'Oh, anything really. I'm not fussy. Since music is all I really know, it's the only way I can think of to earn a little money.'

'Listen, Bianca, if you're broke, I can . . .'

'No,' she broke in hurriedly. 'I'm not broke. I'm okay for now, but I should be earning something. Besides, I'm getting itchy fingers. I'd like to start playing again professionally, preferably with a group of some kind.'

'Well,' he said slowly, 'if you're not fussy, I did get a call from a restaurant right in Malibu a few days ago. They want some strolling gypsy violinists for their dinner crowd.' His voice was apologetic. 'I know that's probably not what you had in mind, but the pay is good, and it's close by. Want to give it a try?'

Bianca thought it over quickly. Tom was right. It wasn't what she'd had in mind at all, but she couldn't afford to be choosy. She knew there weren't that many jobs floating around for unemployed violinists.

'Yes,' she said at last. 'I would like to.'

'Okay. Just a minute and I'll get the address for you. I'll give them a call first and tell them I'm sending you over. Let's say tomorrow morning at eleven.'

'That sounds fine.'

He gave her the address. 'If they've already filled the spot, I'll call you right back, and we'll try to find something else. If not, let me know how it works out.'

'Thanks a million, Tom. I knew I could count on you.'

'Always, Bianca,' he said firmly. 'In every way.'

After they'd hung up, Bianca stood by the telephone for a long time. Strolling gypsy violinist! Quite a switch from the concert hall. She glanced down at the address she had scrawled on the pad by the phone. 'Rumania House,' she murmured aloud. It was on La Cienega Boulevard, one of the main thoroughfares.

She'd never done that kind of work before, but still it might be fun to try. And if it didn't work out, no harm would be done. She felt a little anxious, but also intrigued. She smiled. 'I'm going to have an adventure,' she said aloud.

CHAPTER FIVE

THE next morning Bianca arrived at the Rumania House restaurant promptly at eleven o'clock. She was dressed sedately in a businesslike beige linen suit and sensible bone-coloured pumps. Except for one persistent cowlick in the back, her unruly black hair had for once decided to behave, and she felt that at least she would make a good impression on her potential employer.

It had been an easy place to find on the busy boulevard, and although the front of the restaurant was unprepossessing, once she had parked Laura's BMW in the wide parking lot and gone inside, she was instantly charmed.

The decor and atmosphere were decidedly old-world, she thought as she wandered through the foyer looking for signs of life. A sign on the front window had said they didn't open for dinner until five o'clock, but the door had been unlocked.

She found her way to the dining room, which turned out to be a series of small rooms separated by white latticework partitions and trailing green plants. There were four or five tables in each small section, with squat candles and checked tablecloths on them.

The ceiling was criss-crossed with heavy dark wooden beams that matched the padded leather banquettes and chairs at the tables, and the windows all along one side of the room were of a peculiar smoky glass, opaque and casting a dim interesting light on the interior. Yes, she thought, pleased. Definitely old-world. There was an intimate atmosphere, cozy and warm, which would probably be enhanced at night when the candles were lit.

'Miss Jameson.' She heard a voice call her name and looked up to see a small dark woman walking briskly towards her. She wore a black dress with a heavy pearl necklace around her neck, and her tiny hands flashed from an assortment of brilliant rings. 'I am Madame Tedescu,' she announced.

'Yes,' Bianca replied, moving towards her. 'Mr Schiffren sent me to audition for you.'

The little woman waved a hand in the air. 'No need. If Mr Schiffren says you can play, I know you can play.' She looked Bianca up and down very carefully, the black eyes as bright as buttons in the finely wrinkled face. 'I only want to see what you look like.' her husky voice was heavily accented.

Bianca stood perfectly still, her violin case in her hand, her bag slung over one shoulder. She felt nervous under that penetrating, appraising gaze, but resisted the impulse to squirm. What difference did it make what she looked like? She was a musician, not a dancer.

As if she could read her mind, Madame Tedescu went on briskly. 'You will have to wear a costume, you see.' She cupped her chin in her hand and nodded. 'You'll do, I think, with some make-up. You'll need a wig. Or you can probably pull your hair back, like mine, and I will find a black chignon for you. What are you? A size ten, eight?'

Bianca nodded, totally confused. 'An eight, usually. If it's not too skimpy, that is.'

Madame Tedescu smiled wickedly, wrinkling her wizened face even more. 'Ah, but skimpy is what we want, isn't it? I think an eight. Come, I'll get the costume.' Her voice was brisk, businesslike now. 'Take it home and try it on. If it's impossible, we'll find a larger one tonight. Come with me.'

Stunned, Bianca followed her. She couldn't believe it. The woman hadn't even heard her play. And what was she supposed to play? Wasn't there any music? They were in a tiny, windowless dressing room now. A long metal clothes rack all along one wall was hung with brightly-coloured dresses. Madame Tedescu whipped rapidly through them, took a swath of scarlet satin off a hanger and thrust it at Bianca.

'Be here at six o'clock,' she said. 'That's when our rush hour starts. You will play until midnight, with time out for supper in the kitchen and two fifteen-minute breaks.'

She named a salary. Bianca was impressed. 'But, the music,' she faltered.

The little woman waved a hand in the air. 'The music is simple. Just gypsy airs. Whatever you like. Sarasate. Kreisler. Enesco. You know the kind of thing I mean. There will be two other violinists and an accordionist. They will help you.'

Bianca was still hesitant. It was all happening too fast. Her head was spinning. She looked down at the slinky costume. She wasn't sure she wanted to be on display like that.

'Well?' Madame Tedescu was saying. 'Is there a problem?'

Bianca made up her mind. She needed the money. She wanted to play. And she wanted an adventure, something different. 'No,' she said finally. 'No problem.'

* * *

Her head was still whirling when she arrived back at the beach house after that short, unsettling interview. Her main concern was what she would play. She wished she'd asked Madame Tedescu the names of the other two violinists. If she could at least talk to one of them she might get a better idea of what was expected of her.

She got out of the car, dragging her violin case and costume behind her. That costume! Would it even fit? And what was she going to do with her hair? There was no way she'd be able to make it behave into a sleek chignon. It had a definite mind of its own, and went whichever way it happened to feel like at the moment. Six o'clock! She'd never be ready.

She was halfway to the door, so absorbed in her anxious forebodings that she hadn't even noticed Gerry standing at the group of mailboxes until he called to her.

'Hey, what's up?' Startled out of her brooding, she whirled around to see him ambling casually towards her, a large stack of mail in his hands, a concerned expression on his face.

She forced out a smile. 'It's a long story.' Somehow, his very presence reassured her. She couldn't imagine anything upsetting his equilibrium, and right now she needed that kind of strength. 'Come on in, and I'll tell you about it.'

He followed her inside. 'Do you want some lunch?' she called over her shoulder, moving towards the kitchen. She was suddenly ravenous.

'Sounds good.'

She set her violin case, costume and shoulder bag down on the kitchen counter and turned to face him. He was lounging casually up against the door frame, his arms crossed over his broad chest, looking tanned and relaxed and comforting in his worn jeans and white knit shirt.

'I've got a job,' she announced.

He pushed himself away from the wall and walked slowly towards her, dark eyes alight. 'That's great, Bianca. But why the long face?'

She bit her lip and lowered her eyes. 'I've got the jitters.' She looked up at him. 'It's all happened so fast.' She told him about the job, Rumania House, Madame Tedescu. When she had finished, she spread her arms in a helpless gesture. 'She was so vague about everything. I don't even know what to play.'

He was grinning now, his even white teeth flashing against his tanned face. 'You've got a problem, kid.' He chuckled deep in his throat and reached out a forefinger to touch her lightly on the nose.

'What's so funny?' she snapped, backing away. 'Some help you are.'

'Oh, I'll help you.' He chuckled again, totally unconcerned at her growing anger. 'But I'll have to admit I enjoy seeing you ruffled. You come on so cool and controlled all the time that it does my black heart good to see you're only human after all.'

'Oh, I'm human, all right,' she retorted. 'You're the one with nerves of steel.' She had to smile. 'I thought you'd be a tower of strength to lean on in my moment of crisis, and all you do is laugh at me.'

He eyed her carefully. 'Is that how you see me, Bianca?' he asked gently. 'A tower of strength?'

She ran a hand nervously through her short dark hair. 'Well, I at least thought you'd *try* to help,' she replied lightly, evading the probing question.

'I said I'd help you. Why don't you fix us a sandwich or something while I run next door and look through some old music I've got stored there.'

She stared. 'Music? What kind of music?'

He shrugged. 'I told you I'd done a little bit of everything before I started writing. I used to play piano in a combo. Many long years ago.'

She stood open-mouthed. Was there no end to the surprises this man could spring on her? 'You make yourself sound ancient, Gerry,' she said slowly.

'Not in years, maybe,' was the curt reply. 'I'm thirty-two. But my vast and varied experience of life started at a very tender age.' He put his hands on her shoulders and turned her around to face the kitchen counter. 'Come on, now, get cracking with that lunch. I'll just be a few minutes.'

As he turned away from her to leave, his hand shot out and gave her bottom a light playful smack. She drew in her breath sharply and turned to confront him, but all she saw was his retreating back as he ambled jauntily out of the kitchen.

'That man!' she muttered through clenched teeth. But she had to admit she was feeling much better. Although his light-hearted, playful attitude was aggravating, even infuriating at times, it did serve to put things in a more realistic perspective. She had no idea how he intended to help her, but she was certain it would be another surprise.

Feeling uncomfortable in the beige linen suit, she decided to change her clothes before she tackled lunch. She glanced with distaste at the sleazy red costume still sitting crumpled on the drainingboard, and her heart sank. She'd have to face that, too, eventually. Later, she promised herself. With a sigh and a roll of her eyes, she gathered up the costume and went into the bedroom. When she hung it up, she cringed at the low-cut bodice. What had she got herself into?

By the time Gerry returned, carrying a stack of tattered sheet music, she had already changed into jeans and a cotton shirt and was slicing tuna sandwiches.

'You found something!' she called as he breezed into the kitchen, brandishing the music.

'I told you I would,' he chided, peering over her shoulder at the sandwiches. 'Looks good. I'm starved.'

'Let me see,' she said, reaching for the music. While she leafed through it, Gerry got down a glass from the cupboard over the sink and went to the refrigerator for some milk.

'Want some?' he asked, lifting the carton.

'Please,' she murmured. The music looked simple enough. Two of Lizst's Hungarian Rhapsodies, Zigeuner, some Enesco, and, of course, Brahms' Hungarian Dances.

She looked at Gerry. He was leaning against the counter, chewing thoughtfully, making himself right at home. She watched as he took a long swallow of milk then wiped his mouth on the back of his hand.

'Got any pickles?' he asked politely. 'Potato chips?'

'I'm surprised you haven't already found them,' she said dryly.

'Oh, I don't like to push,' he rejoined modestly, lowering his eyes.

She had to laugh. She *was* grateful to him, after

all. 'Gerry, this music is wonderful, just the thing for a strolling gypsy violinist.'

'Right,' he said with satisfaction. 'Eat up, now, and we'll run through it.'

She shook her head. 'I can't eat. I'm too nervous.'

'Eat, I said,' he ordered sternly. 'How can you stroll properly tonight without sustenance? Go on, eat.' He reached across, picked up half her sandwich and thrust it at her.

'Oh, all right,' she said, taking it and forcing down a bite.

He reached for the other half. 'But so long as you're not hungry, I might as well finish up your sandwich. Don't want to waste food. Think of the starving children in Greece.'

She stared. 'What starving children in Greece? Children don't starve in Greece.'

He shrugged. 'I don't know. That's what my mother used to tell us when we were kids and wouldn't eat our carrots.'

'And then you ate your carrots?'

He shook his head, grinning, his mouth full of *her* tuna sandwich. He swallowed. 'No way. I still can't stand them. I told her to send them to the children in Greece if she was so worried about them.'

She eyed him wryly. 'I'll bet you were just as impossible when you were a little boy as you are now.'

He nodded. 'You're right.'

'Your poor mother!'

He laughed shortly. 'My poor mother is now living in a luxury condo in Florida, thanks to her impossible son.'

Bianca was touched, but also confused. Her

visions of Gerry as a struggling writer living off the generosity of his friends in Japan were slowly fading. He had offered to loan—no, *give*—her money. She eyed him carefully. He had turned away from her and was rinsing out his glass at the kitchen sink. She took in the shabby jeans, moulding his firm muscular hips and thighs like a second skin. The white knit shirt, stretching tautly over his broad shoulders as he leaned forward over the sink, had definitely seen better days. He badly needed a haircut, and the white sneakers on his feet were worn almost beyond repair.

He was an enigma to her, a puzzle, and this made her vaguely uncomfortable. She had sensed from the beginning of their friendship that he was hiding something from her. On the surface, he seemed absolutely open, frank and sincere. Yet she was intuitively aware that there were hidden depths to this unusual man, so pleasant and boyish in some ways, yet so secretive and withdrawn in others.

He was drying his hands now on the towel he'd found inside the cupboard under the sink, and she watched as he folded it neatly and returned it to the rod fastened to the door.

As though he had sensed her troubled gaze on him all the while, he turned slowly to her and once again ran a finger lightly down her nose.

'Don't worry about it, Bianca,' he said softly. 'I just want to be your friend. I like you. And I'll never hurt you.'

She was gazing now directly into those mysterious dark eyes of his, fathomless pools of liquid brown, almost black. She sensed behind them a wealth of experience, a solid self-confidence, and yet, too, the merest hint of pain.

'Come on,' he said abruptly, taking the music from her. 'Let's get started. You've only got a few hours.'

She followed him into the living room, still immersed in her speculations about this strange man. She took out her violin and went to the piano. He was sitting there, the music spread out on the rack, leafing through it. While she mechanically tuned the instrument, her thoughts were still on Gerry.

Why shouldn't she trust him? She believed him when he said he'd never hurt her. He was a tease, and he was arrogant, but there didn't seem to be a malicious bone in his body. There was no reason why they couldn't be friends. After those first few blatant attempts he'd made to seduce her, he'd backed off when she'd made it clear that wasn't what she wanted. And they'd been pretty feeble efforts. He hadn't pushed her, had never forced anything on her.

Perversely, she wondered now if he didn't find her attractive enough, desirable enough, to make an ardent pursuit worth his while. She wondered dimly, too, if she hadn't made a mistake not to encourage that pursuit. A man like Gerry didn't come along every day of the week. He was simply the most splendid physical specimen she'd ever encountered. Besides that, he was nice, he was fun to be with, and he seemed to have a serious purpose in life with his writing. He wasn't a mere playboy or beach bum as she'd first suspected.

Could she attract him again if she put her mind to it? Then it came back to her in a flash why she had rejected his advances in the first place. This was no schoolboy she was dealing with, in spite of his playful ways. He was a widely experienced man. She would be like putty in his hands if she ever allowed herself to even *think* of him in terms more intimate than a casual friendship, much less actually lead him on.

He was playing softly, expertly, a haunting Lizst rhapsody, and she listened, astounded at his expertise. He was far from a concert performer, but his touch was sure, his sense of chord structure near-perfect, and even the simplified version he was playing of the diabolically difficult music had a professional ring to it.

All business now, he glanced up at her. 'Ready?' he asked. She nodded, and they began to play.

By five o'clock, they'd got in three solid hours of practice, and Bianca was feeling much more secure about the music. Once she got the idea, it was a simple matter, far easier than concert playing. It was just a different style, a different approach, and she was a thorough enough musician to be able to fake it once she knew what was expected.

When Gerry pointed out the time and told her she'd better start getting ready if she had to be at the restaurant by six, she gasped in disbelief, and immediately her anxieties returned. She gave Gerry one stricken look.

'I can't do it,' she announced.

He was still seated at the piano and had turned around on the bench to look up at her. 'What do you mean, you can't do it? You did great.'

She waved her bow nervously in the air. 'Oh, it's not the music, it's the people, the costume.' She groaned. 'I haven't even tried it on.'

He glanced at his watch. 'Well, you'd better go do it now or you'll never make it in time. Go put it on, and I'll give you my expert opinion.'

'No!' she cried. She didn't want him to see her in that skimpy red dress. 'No,' she repeated firmly. 'I appreciate your help this afternoon, but I want you to leave now so I can get ready.'

'Are you sure?' he asked. She nodded. 'Okay.' He got up from the piano and flexed his cramped fingers. 'I'll see you tonight, then.'

'What?' She stared at him, aghast.

'I said I'll see you tonight.' He grinned. 'I wouldn't miss your debut for the world.' He began to hum a few bars of *The Gypsy Love Song*, his warm dark eyes teasing.

'Gerry,' she said firmly, 'I want you to promise me you won't ever, ever come to Rumania House when I'm playing.'

His dark eyebrows shot up. 'Come on, Bianca, don't be like that. Why not?'

She was becoming frantic. She'd die if he saw her in that costume. It was getting late. She had to get moving. 'Gerry, promise me!' she cried, on the verge of hysteria. What if the costume didn't fit? What about make-up? She didn't know anything about make-up. And her hair! Oh, Lord, her hair! She ran a hand distractedly through it now, virtually beside herself with anxiety.

'Okay, okay,' Gerry said calmly, aware now of her distress. 'I promise I won't come to the restaurant tonight.' He started towards the door. 'It'll be okay, honey,' he called softly. 'I'll come over tomorrow and you can tell me how it went.'

She managed a tremulous smile. 'Thank you, Gerry,' she said fervently. 'For everything.'

By some miracle she managed to get to the restaurant before six, even taking into account the five minutes she'd spent aganising in front of the mirror in the bedroom after she'd put on that hated red costume. Actually, it fitted quite well, and even though it was cut a little low in front for her taste and was virtually backless, it wasn't nearly as bad as she'd anticipated.

What appalled her was the fact that the material was so thin and slinky that every ridge and seam and strap of her underwear stood out under it in sharp relief. She tried a strapless bra, but that didn't work because the dress was cut so low in the back. She tried it again without the bra, twisting this way and that in front of the mirror to get the full effect. Although definitely not flat-chested, her breasts were high and firm, and the revealing cleavage between them was pretty tame. The seconds ticked by. She had to make up her mind. Finally, with a sigh, she decided to go without the bra. Then, in a frenzy, she put on the sheerest, filmiest pair of tights she owned, slipped her feet into a pair of high-heeled black sandals, and decided she'd just have to do.

At the restaurant, with her costume at least half-covered by a light raincoat, her violin clutched in her hand, she made her way through the main dining area and back to the tiny dressing room as unobtrusively as possible. There were only a few scattered customers as yet, but it was a Friday night and the restaurant would probably be packed later.

As she slipped into the dressing room, she heard someone call her name. 'Oh, Miss Jameson. Bianca.' It was Madame Tedescu, bearing down on her from the direction of the kitchen. 'You are early. That is good.'

Bianca smiled nervously at her new employer. She was still wearing the same black dress and heavy pearl necklace, but tonight her face was heavily made-up. Even in the dim light of the narrow hallway, Bianca could see the thick layer of powder that barely covered the deep wrinkles in that sharp little face.

She gave Bianca an appraising look with her bright button eyes. 'You have on your costume, I see.' Bianca nodded and the tiny woman gave her a closer look. 'Tsk, tsk,' she clucked, 'but no make-up.' She frowned. 'And your hair. Ach, it will not do at all.' She pushed open the door. 'Come. I will help you just this once.'

She switched on the bright overhead light and sat Bianca down at a shabby dressing table that was literally covered with jars, boxes, bottles and tubes of every size and description. Bianca gazed at her reflection in the cracked mirror. Her face seemed naked to her compared to Madame Tedescu's, even though she had put on a little rosy lipstick and black mascara.

'Take your coat off.' Bianca obeyed.

Without another word, the woman set to work on Bianca's face and hair. Foundation, a heavy liquid make-up base, blusher, eyeliner, eyebrow pencil. She worked swiftly and silently, muttering occasionally to herself as though Bianca wasn't even there. Gradually, she saw her thin 'interesting' face transformed into a garish mask. Her dark eyes seemed huge, with impossibly long lashes and heavy brows. The bright slash of lipstick on her mouth and rouged cheeks completed the picture, and Bianca felt as though she no longer existed. Some Las Vegas showgirl had suddenly appeared in her place.

She turned to Madame Tedescu to protest, but at that moment the door opened and two other women burst into the room. One was dark, heavyset, middle-aged, the other blonde, thinner and much younger. They both carried violin cases.

'Good evening, ladies,' Madame said. 'This is Bianca, our new violinist. Diane and Barbara will tell you what to do.' She gazed into the mirror, squinting her eyes, as she surveyed Bianca's appearance. 'Good,' she said with satisfaction. 'Your own mother wouldn't know you. Now, the hair.'

The protest died on Bianca's lips. The woman had a point. Of course, her family and friends would probably recognise her, but the heavy make-up did constitute a sort of disguise, and when Madame pulled her hair back tightly off her forehead and pinned on a thick, black chignon, the transformation was complete.

Gazing at her new image in the mirror, she saw that Bianca Jameson had indeed disappeared, to be replaced by a sultry-eyed, flamboyant gypsy girl. Her spirits rose. She felt far more confident now that she could go through with it. As far as the patrons of the restaurant were concerned, she wouldn't even be Bianca Jameson.

'Now,' Madame was saying, 'it is almost time. From now on,' she went on sternly, 'you must do all this yourself, Bianca.'

She scurried out of the room, then, and taking one last look in the mirror and making a tiny adjustment to the heavy chignon, Bianca stood up and faced the other two women.

After some hesitation and a few awkward moments out in the dining room, the evening went smoothly. At first, Bianca watched Barbara and Diane carefully to see how they handled themselves. The male accordionist, who looked like a real gypsy, with a twirling black moustache, swarthy complexion and flashing dark eyes, would accompany each girl in turn, and as time went on, Bianca found herself recalling quite easily the music she and Gerry had practised that afternoon.

By the time she had her supper break at eight o'clock, she was exhausted. It was tiring enough to play even simple music for two hours straight, but even worse when she had to be constantly on the move, strolling from table to table.

She wolfed down the plate of spicy goulash she was served in the busy kitchen, then with a sigh, leaned back in her chair and made her body go limp. Flexing her cramped fingers, she slipped off the uncomfortable sandals and wiggled her toes, her legs stretched out in front of her. Lord, she was tired. She closed her eyes.

'Sorry, Bianca,' came a low voice in her ear, 'it's time to get back. Recess is over.'

Her eyes flew open, and she looked up to see Barbara leaning over her, a sympathetic look on her round, kind face. 'So soon?' Bianca groaned.

Barbara gave her a friendly grin. 'The first week is rough, but when you get used to it it won't be so bad.'

Bianca stood up and stretched, arching her aching back. 'I hope you're right,' she muttered as she slipped back into the sandals. She picked up her violin and tuned it, then with a rueful grin at Barbara, started back to the dining room.

'One thing you should watch out for,' Barbara called softly, 'especially on weekends. Later on, some of the serious drinkers may get a little amorous. Nothing serious, and you don't want to offend the paying customers.' She grinned. 'One of the advantages of strolling is that you're always on the move. In case you do have a problem, though, just give a shout for Dino, the accordionist. He's also the bouncer.'

'Thanks for the warning,' Bianca said weakly. Barbara gave her a little salute and turned to her supper.

Shutting the kitchen door behind her, Bianca took a deep breath and began to move towards the dining area, dodging bustling waiters laden with precariously balanced trays and searching for Dino. His accompaniment was a big help. She finally spotted him far across the room and began to walk towards him. As she passed by a noisy group at a large table in the middle of one of the dining areas, she felt a hand grasp her wrist.

She looked down at a fat, middle-aged man who was grinning up at her and brandishing a five dollar bill in his hand. Recalling Barbara's warning, she smiled sweetly down at him and deftly slid her arm out of his grasp.

'Yes, sir,' she said politely, instantly on guard.

'It's our anniversary,' he said tipsily, nodding at the grey-haired woman seated beside him. 'Can you play *Gypsy Love Song* for us?'

'Of course,' she replied, relaxing. Since he was still poking the bill at her, she took it from him and thanked him with a smile. She debated for a moment, then tucked it into the bosom of her red costume, the only conceivable place it would go. Then she lifted her bow and began to play. It was one of the pieces she and Gerry had practised that afternoon, and as she played she closed her eyes and tried to imagine that he was there accompanying her.

When the last lingering strains of the sweet melody had hushed to a close, Bianca heard a loud round of applause and opened her eyes, blinking at the sudden sound and the lights of the flickering candles. She collected herself, smiled and bowed, then moved on.

When she got home that night, well after midnight, she had just enough strength to wash off the heavy make-up, put on her nightgown and fall into bed. She was asleep the moment her head hit the pillow and barely stirred until the ringing of the telephone awakened her the next morning.

Blinking and stretching, she groaned and rolled over to see what time it was. The sun was pouring in through the bedroom window, and she saw by the clock on the nightstand that it was after nine o'clock. The phone continued to ring. Groggily, she rolled out of bed, every muscle in her body aching, and stumbled into the living room to answer it.

'Hello,' she mumbled.

'Well? How did it go?' It was Tom. She cleared her throat and flopped down in a nearby chair.

'Not bad. In fact, quite well. I'm just tired.'

'It's gruelling work,' Tom said in a soothing tone. 'I know. I did the same thing in my student days in New York.'

Bianca perked up. 'Did you really?'

'I sure did. In those days I jumped at the chance to perform anywhere they'd pay me.'

'And you actually lived to tell the tale?' she asked with a groan. 'I feel as though I've been put through a meat grinder.'

He chuckled. 'You'll survive. Wait and see. In a week you'll be an old hand at the game. It's just a matter of getting used to a new routine, new music, new surroundings . . . '

'And new muscles,' she broke in. 'I didn't even know I had so many places to hurt.'

'Well, yes, there's that, too. Listen, I thought I'd stop by the restaurant for dinner tonight to catch your act.'

She thought about that skimpy costume. 'Oh, Tom, I don't know. I wish you wouldn't. I'd be embarrassed.'

'Whyever for? I'm your teacher, remember? Surely the music can't be that difficult for you?'

'It's not the music,' she explained carefully. 'It's everything else. The way I look. Most of all the costume. It's—ah—not my usual style.'

'Bianca,' he said sternly. 'This is Tom. I've known you since you were twelve years old. You're not going to go all shy on me now, are you?'

She pondered his question. In spite of the crush she'd had on him, their relationship had always been more like uncle and niece or brother and sister. Her oldest brother, Tony, was about Tom's age, and it wouldn't bother her to have Tony see her in her gypsy role.

'Well, all right,' she said finally. 'If you really want to Maybe you can give me some expert criticism.'

He laughed. 'I doubt that. See you this evening, then.'

After they hung up, Bianca went back to her room to shower and dress. Soaking under the pelting spray, as hot as she could stand it, she thought over her conversation with Tom. She wasn't crazy about the idea of having him come to the restaurant to watch her play, but at least he wasn't Gerry. Now *that* she couldn't tolerate.

As she dried herself and brushed out her damp hair, she wondered what the difference was. Why couldn't she even bear to think about the possibility of Gerry seeing her in that costume? He had quit making amorous advances to her. They were only friends. She pictured him in her mind sitting at one of the tables in the dining room, the dark secretive eyes on her as she strolled by in the low-cut, backless red dress, skin tight, with virtually nothing on underneath it, and shivered involuntarily. No way, she thought firmly.

She dressed quickly in a pair of white shorts that set off her tanned legs and a pale blue halter top. In the living room, she slid open the glass door and stepped out on to the verandah. It was a beautiful day. The weather had settled into a typical Southern Californian spring now that April had arrived. She'd been at the beach for three months now and was finally growing accustomed to the dependable sunshine. Here in Malibu the ocean breezes kept the smog at bay, and every morning was a revelation of blue, blue sky and balmy weather.

Over a light breakfast she decided that a brisk walk up the beach would loosen more of the kinks in her aching joints and muscles. Then she'd lie in the sun for a while and later on run through her music again. She was just finishing her second cup of coffee when she heard a light tapping on the open door leading out to the verandah.

'Anybody home?' came a familiar cheerful voice.

'In here, Gerry,' she called from the kitchen.

She was sitting at the round, glass-topped table in the corner of the room near the window, and looked up as he appeared in the doorway. He was dressed in his dark bathing trunks and a loose, short-sleeved cotton shirt. Lounging back against the doorframe he gave her an enquiring look.

'Well? How did it go?'

She was surpised at how glad she was to see him, and realised suddenly how she had looked forward to his coming over today, even counted on it. She stared up at him, her throat oddly constricted. He was so darned appealing, she thought, from the smooth thick hair on his fine, arrogant head to the lithe tanned body beneath it. All glorious male animal, he sent messages of almost blatant sensuality just standing still.

'Well?' he repeated with a grin. 'Are you going to answer me or are you going to stare at me all day?'

Reddening, she dropped her eyes and took a quick swallow of coffee to cover her confusion. He was well aware, she thought, of the reason for her open appraisal. 'Sorry,' she muttered. 'I'm not quite with it yet this morning.' She took another swallow of coffee. Steadier now, she smiled back at him. 'It went fine. A little gruelling physically, but I think I'll get used to it.'

He was ambling towards her now. When he reached the table, he turned a chair around and straddled it, folded his arms over the top and leaned his chin on them.

'Got any more coffee?'

'Yes, of course.' She got up to pour him a cup. It was only Gerry, she thought as she handed him his coffee. He was just being friendly. Then why was her heart pounding so? She sat down opposite him.

'Tell me about it,' he said.

As she related the events of her first night on the

job, she relaxed more and more. He seemed to be really interested, laughing at her description of Madame Tedescu, frowning at Barbara's warning about grabby patrons.

'And did you have any problem along those lines?' he asked.

She shook her head. 'Not so far. I was a little concerned once.' She told him about the tipsy middle-aged man and his anniversary request. 'But when I discovered his wife was right there, I knew there wouldn't be any problem. Besides, Dino would have come to my rescue if I'd really needed help.'

He frowned, his cup halfway to his mouth. 'Who's Dino?'

'The accordionist. Also the bouncer. A dark gypsy type.'

He was silent as he slowly lifted the mug and drank his coffee. 'Bianca,' he said finallly, his tone light, 'I really do want to come and see you play.'

Her face clouded. 'Please don't, Gerry.' She made a helpless gesture with her hands. 'I guess I'm being silly, but I feel so—so exposed in that awful costume. When Tom called this morning and said he was coming to the restaurant tonight, I almost wouldn't let him come, either.'

'What do you mean, "almost"?' he asked evenly.

Bianca looked up at the hint of menace in his voice. She shrugged. 'Well, you know, it's only Tom. I wasn't too crazy about the idea, but . . .' She broke off and stared.

He had risen to his feet and was leaning over the table, his palms braced flat against it, his dark eyes blazing. She had never seen him look really angry before, and she decided instantly that she didn't like it. The latent menace she had always sensed in him seemed suddenly to have erupted to the surface.

'I see,' he said in that same even tone. 'Tom can see you. Dino can see you. Every middle-aged lecher in Southern California can see you. But *I* can't see you. Is that it?'

'Gerry, I . . .' she stumbled.

For a long moment their eyes remained locked together. His hostility emanated towards her in waves as he glared down at her. Her throat and mouth were dry, and she nervously ran her tongue over her lips.

'Hell!' he muttered and straightened up. 'I thought we were friends, Bianca.' He forced out a smile. 'Who was it who coached you yesterday and taught you how to be a proper gypsy?' He shook his head and sighed. 'Oh, come on. Don't look so stricken. I won't eat you. I shouldn't have yelled at you like that, but, damn it, you can be stubborn when you want to.'

She was so relieved to see him smiling again that she slumped back in her chair limply. 'Please try to understand, Gerry,' she said at last. 'I do appreciate your help. I couldn't have managed without it. It's just that I feel so—so *exposed* in that awful costume and all that silly make-up. It's not *me*.'

'Okay, okay. Forget it. Get up.' She hesitated, unsure of what he wanted. 'Come on. I can spare an hour or two this morning for some coaching. After that, I've got to hit the book and you're on your own.'

Slowly she rose to her feet. 'I feel guilty taking up so much of your time, Gerry,' she said. 'You've got your own work to do.'

He reached out and grabbed her arm. 'I

wouldn't do it if I didn't want to.' He flung an arm around her shoulders and guided her to the piano in the living room. He sat down on the bench and played a few chords, then looked up at her. 'Friends?' he asked softly.

She nodded. 'Friends.'

CHAPTER SIX

BIANCA'S second night of playing at Rumania House did indeed go much more smoothly than the first. Although she still fell exhausted into a chair in the kitchen at her supper break, at least she knew now what was expected of her. She had even applied her own make-up that evening when she arrived, sticking at the unfamiliar task with awkward fingers until she got Barbara's smiling approval.

Her playing was more assured tonight, too. She and Gerry had practised some new music, and as she strolled among the tables with her violin, she found herself genuinely enjoying her job. The haunting gypsy airs were not her usual style, but there was a poignant beauty to them that evoked in Bianca the warm response of a true musician to any good music. She expecially liked to play the tune, *When A Gypsy Makes His Violin Cry*, and since that was exactly the effect she aimed at, she decided to make it her theme song.

The patrons were well-behaved and responded warmly to her playing. She received several tips when she played special requests, all duly tucked into the bodice of her costume. She found she quite enjoyed the intimacy of the cozy dining areas. It was a new experience for her, accustomed as she was to the separation from her audience of the concert stage.

She had forgotten all about Tom's intention to eat at the restaurant tonight until she resumed playing after her supper break. She had just finished playing a wickedly difficult Sarasate piece for a family group celebrating a birthday and was smiling and nodding at the appreciative applause when she felt a hand on her arm. She turned swiftly around, prepared to ease herself out of a sticky situation, and saw Tom smiling at her. He was seated at the table right behind her with another man across from him.

Her eyes lit up. 'Tom. You did come.'

He was shaking his head slowly from side to side. 'I'm so glad to see it really is you, Bianca. I hardly recognised you and had visions of getting slapped by a strange woman for getting fresh.'

She laughed. 'Oh, we don't do that here. We have subtler ways of handling grabbers.' She tilted her bow at the burly Dino, who was eyeing her carefully from across the room.

'Yes, I see,' Tom said. 'It seems you're well protected. Can you sit down a minute?'

'I guess so. I haven't taken either of my short breaks yet. If it's against the rules to mingle with the paying customers, I'm sure Madame Tedescu will let me know.'

She slid on to the leather padded banquette beside him and glanced briefly at the man sitting across from him. He was one of the handsomest men she had ever seen, with shaggy, but well-cut thick blond hair, even white teeth smiling in a heavily tanned face and dazzling blue eyes.

She smiled hesitantly at him, then turned to Tom, waiting to see if he intended to introduce them. There was a strange look of intensity on her friend's face. He was simply staring at her, a baffled look in his eyes.

'Tom?' she said softly.

He jumped and reddened. ‘Sorry,’ he muttered. ‘I just can’t get over your appearance.’

‘Is it that bad?’

He shook his head. ‘Not bad at all. Just so different. I’m not used to seeing you as a *femme fatale*.’ He looked at his companion. ‘Bianca, this is Bruce Holloway. Bruce, Bianca Jameson, my star pupil.’

‘How do you do,’ Bianca murmured.

The man flashed a brilliant smile at her and returned her greeting. ‘A pleasure,’ he said in a low throaty voice. ‘I enjoyed your playing very much.’

Bianca thanked him and turned back to Tom. ‘Well, what do you think, teacher? Will I pass as a gypsy violinist? I’m thinking of making it my career.’

Tom was still giving her the oddest look. He glanced at Bruce Holloway, his mouth twitching as though he was trying hard not to laugh. A look passed between the two men. Tom turned back to Bianca with a wide grin. Something funny was going on, she thought. It was as though they were enjoying some huge private joke at her expense. Flustered, she toyed nervously with the violin bow in her lap.

Apparently reading her thoughts, Tom reached out to cover her hand with his. ‘You did great, Bianca. You really made your fiddle sing. I think you have a great future as a gypsy.’

Bianca smiled. ‘I’m not sure I could stand the pace, but it is fun, and the pay is marvellous. I even get tips.’

At that moment two teenage girls approached their table. One of them cleared her throat nervously and gave Bruce Holloway an adoring glance. 'Mr Holloway,' she said shyly, 'could we please have your autograph?'

'Certainly,' he said in an easy, practised drawl, and reached for the pieces of paper the girls were holding out to him.

Immediately, two older women and a young boy appeared behind the girls, staring at Bruce and clutching odd scraps of paper in their hands. Bianca stared at the tableau before her, and while Bruce was occupied with signing and chatting easily to his admirers, she turned to Tom with a puzzled frown.

'What's going on?' she whispered.

'You mean you really don't know?' he asked in a stunned tone. She shook her head. Tom leaned towards her and spoke into her ear in a low voice. 'Bruce Holloway just happens to be the hottest thing in movies since Robert Redford.'

Bianca's eyes widened. 'You mean he's a movie star?' Tom nodded, and Bianca put her hand to her forehead in a gesture of dismay. 'Oh, Tom,' she breathed, 'how awful! He must think I'm a terrible klutz not to recognise him. I don't know anything about the movies.' She wasn't even that sure who Robert Redford was, for that matter, although she had a dim recollection that he was very famous.

'I think he found it refreshing.' He motioned with his head. 'Take a look.'

Bianca glanced across the table to see the forced smile on Bruce Holloway's handsome face, the glazed look in the blue eyes, the firm set of his mouth. He was smiling, but his eyes were grim, as though he was forcing himself to be pleasant under great stress.

When the last autograph-seeker had left, the

blond man turned to Bianca and Tom. He looked so drained, Bianca thought, his face ashen under the tan, the eyes dead and empty of the spark she had seen before.

He shrugged and lit a cigarette with shaky fingers. 'Sorry about that,' he muttered, exhaling a stream of smoke in a heavy sigh. 'I can't seem to escape it.'

'Why do you do it?' Bianca asked softly. 'You could have said no, turned them away.'

He shrugged again and inhaled deeply. 'It's my bread and butter.' He gave her a rueful smile. 'I've become public property. They pay to see my films. I can at least put my name on a piece of paper for them.'

Bianca shivered a little. 'It sounds awful,' she said in a tone of genuine pity.

Tom threw his head back and laughed. 'Don't waste your sympathy on Bruce,' he said at last. 'I knew him back when he was a struggling young actor. Ask him to tell you about his mansion in Beverly Hills, his beach house in Acapulco, his Rolls Royce, his yacht, and all those adoring women.'

Bianca glanced warily at Bruce. He was smiling now, more relaxed. 'Well, yes,' he admitted. 'There is that, too.'

Madame Tedescu appeared just then at their table, her piercing black button eyes fastened on Bianca. 'Good evening, Tom,' she said sweetly. 'Mr Holloway.'

Bianca got hurriedly to her feet. 'Well, my break is over,' she said to Tom. 'I'd better get back to work.' She turned to Bruce Holloway. 'It was nice to meet you, Mr Holloway,' she said politely.

He rose to his feet and took her hand. 'The

pleasure was all mine, Bianca.' He gave the hand a warm squeeze, then released it and looked directly into her eyes. 'I'm sure we'll meet again.'

What in the world did he mean by that remark? Bianca wondered as she moved slowly back among the tables and propped her violin under her chin. As she strolled around, playing mechanically, she thought about the meeting. A famous movie star! And she didn't even recognise him! A devastatingly attractive man, she thought, but something about him bothered her. He reminded her of an unpleasant association, even a threatening one.

It wasn't until she was drifting off to sleep that night in her own bed, exhausted again from her evening's labours, that she made the connection. He reminded her of the way Gerry had acted when she first knew him, she realised hazily, on the verge of unconsciousness. The studied poses, the arrogance, the practised movements, all the little things she had noticed in her neighbour that had bothered her about him at first and kept her on guard against him for so long.

Her last thought as she slipped into oblivion was that Gerry wasn't like that any more, at least not with her.

In the days that followed, Bianca fell easily into a comfortable routine. The days passed pleasantly, and by the time she had been on the job for two weeks, she felt like a pro. The gypsy costume still bothered her, but the heavy make-up and elaborate fake chignon did constitute a disguise, and when she performed now, it was easy to forget who she was.

She still, however, steadfastly refused to allow

Gerry to come to the restaurant to watch her play. She didn't know why. It wouldn't have bothered her if anyone else she knew saw her there, but she didn't want him.

It had become a habit by now for them to spend a large part of the day with each other. It had started with their daily practice sessions and soon extended to long walks along the beach, a swim in the surf, a leisurely chat out on the sunny verandah, and then even to sharing their dinners on Bianca's two nights off a week.

She had asked him one day to let her read his book, and when he finally did, after some hesitation, she was deeply impressed by his use of language and the scope of his knowledge and experience of life.

The hero of the novel was a young actor with high ideals who had become corrupted by the movies' system of exploitation and eventually committed suicide. Gerry's terse portrayal of the whole Hollywood scene was vivid and dramatic, even devastating in its sharp condemnation. As she read it, she thought about his comments early in their acquaintance about the free-and-easy lifestyle he had lived and his desire to wean himself away from it.

Occasionally, when they were swimming, or sitting quietly listening to music, or seated across from each other at the kitchen table, Bianca would surprise a peculiar look in his dark eyes, a strange, appraising stare, although their relationship was growing closer each day, there had been no repetition of those early 'attacks' she had complained of, yet he was, indeed, a very affectionate man. He liked her, she knew, and she was drawn to him more all the time, even came to depend on seeing him every day. It was commonplace now for him to take her hand or slip an arm around her shoulder as they walked together along the beach, and whenever he left her, it was with a little hug and a quick peck on the cheek.

Although there were times she found herself wanting more, when she found it hard to resist the desire to reach out her hand and touch him, she was content with the way things were. She still sensed danger in him, in those brooding looks that appeared from time to time on his handsome face, the way he moved, like a jungle cat ready to spring, and the occasional lingering touch of his hand on her arm.

She would laugh at herself then and relax once again. They were good friends, but that's all either of them wanted. His early attempts at seduction were made more from habit than desire, she was sure, and he obviously no longer saw her as potential prey.

She had forgotten all about her meeting with Bruce Holloway until she and Gerry were sitting out on the verandah enjoying a cold drink one warm Sunday after another practice session, and the telephone rang.

She got up from the chaise and stepped inside to the living room to answer it, excusing herself to Gerry, who was sprawled in a canvas-backed chair improving his tan.

'Hello.'

'Bianca?' came a strange throaty masculine voice. 'This is Bruce Holloway.'

She drew in her breath sharply. 'Oh.' She was so startled she didn't know what to say to him.

He chuckled deep in his throat. 'Such response overwhelms me.'

'I'm sorry—ah—Bruce. I'm just . . . I mean . . .' She collected herself and went on more firmly. 'I'm just surprised to hear from you, that's all.'

'I said we'd meet again. I understand you have Sunday night off. If you have no other plans, I'd like to take you out to dinner tonight.'

Bianca was speechless. He wanted to take her out to dinner. How did he know she had Sunday night off? Tom knew. He must have told him. What should she do? He was a movie star, for heaven's sake. What did he want from her? She was very flattered, but did she want to go out with him? She thought of the line of autograph-seekers and the devastating, practised charm of the man.

'Bianca?' came his voice. 'Are you there?'

'Yes, Bruce. Yes, I'm still here.' Her mind raced. 'Uh, Bruce, I don't think that's such a good idea. I mean, I'm not what you think I am.' She rushed on. 'I'm really a very ordinary person. That costume, the make-up. That's not me at all. I'm just a musician, not a showgirl.'

'I don't know what you're talking about,' came the deep warm voice. 'But we can discuss it tonight over dinner.'

For a moment she was tempted. Then she remembered. 'I can't tonight,' she said. 'I have other plans.' She had promised to make a pizza for Gerry. 'Maybe some other time,' she added weakly.

'I'll be out of town for the next few months on location,' he replied smoothly. 'Break your date and come with me tonight.'

'No, I can't do that,' she said firmly. 'I've already promised.'

There was a pause. 'All right, Bianca. Have it your way. But I'll be calling you again.'

After she hung up she stood staring down at the telephone for a long time. What would a man like Bruce Holloway possibly want with her? A man who could probably have his pick of any woman in the world. There was probably a line a mile long panting to get into his bed. Of course, he'd only seen her in her costume and make-up. He had no idea of who she really was, what she was really like.

A shadow suddenly blocked out the sun coming in through the glass door, and she lifted her head to see Gerry standing there, his arms stretched wide and braced against the door frames on either side of him. He was wearing the dark bathing trunks with a short terry-cloth shirt, unzipped down the front for sunbathing, and there was an enquiring look on his face.

'What was all that about?' he asked. 'You seem upset.'

She gazed at him. 'The funniest thing,' she said slowly. 'A few weeks ago at the restaurant Tom introduced me to this man.' She laughed dryly. 'It was so embarrassing. He turned out to be a movie star and I didn't even recognise him.' She gestured helplessly at the telephone. 'He just called to ask me out to dinner tonight.'

Gerry remained quite still, standing there, his long lithe body poised and taut, an inscrutable look on his dark face. 'What's his name?' he said at last.

'Bruce Holloway.'

He began to walk slowly towards her, a strange gleam in the hooded dark eyes. 'And you didn't recognise him,' he stated flatly.

She shook her head. 'Afraid not.' She grinned up at him. 'The last movie I saw was *True Grit*, ten years ago when I was twelve years old.' She shrugged. 'Then they began getting so raunchy, I just quit going. Besides, I was busy with other things. The people I know don't go to movies.'

'Are you going out with him?' He was looking down at her now, standing quite close.

'No. Of course not.'

'Why, of course not?'

'Well, for one thing, I'm going to fix you a pizza tonight.' She smiled at him. 'For another, I'm not interested in seductive movie stars.'

He cocked an eyebrow at that. 'Ah, he was seductive, was he?' His tone was light, but there was a serious note behind it.

She laughed. 'He certainly thought so.' Then she sobered. 'I'm not his type anyway. If anything, he was intrigued by a mysterious gypsy who didn't recognise him. He wouldn't give me—the real Bianca Jameson—a second glance.'

'That must be some costume,' he remarked dryly. 'Well I, for one, prefer this Bianca Jameson.' He gave her a critical look. 'Messy mop of hair, no make-up, baggy clothes and all.'

She glanced down at her loose cotton shirt hanging over an old pair of shorts. 'Why you . . .' she cried, reaching out to give him a shove.

When her hands made contact with the bare flesh of his muscled chest, she drew in her breath sharply as the nerves of her fingers recorded the message of his soft warm skin in her brain. Before she had a chance to put any real muscle into the push, his hands settled on top of hers, holding them and pressing them closely, her palms flat against his chest.

She could feel the quickening beat of his heart under her fingers. His skin was still warm from the sun and slightly damp with perspiration. Slowly, she raised her eyes to his, and her own pulse began to thud erratically. A slow warmth began to steal through her. She swayed slightly. Her mouth felt suddenly dry, and she swallowed convulsively under his dark gaze.

'Bianca,' he said softly, and his head slowly came down towards her.

She closed her eyes, paralysed, unable to move, hardly daring to breathe. When his mouth finally met hers, she couldn't suppress a small, almost inaudible murmur of pleasure. It was nothing like the kisses he had pressed on her before. There was no blatant seductive assault, no thrusting demand, only the delicious taste of his soft sensuous lips moving gently, coaxingly on hers.

But neither was it merely a friendly kiss. The waves of heated response flowing through her told her that, and when one large hand slipped behind her waist and pulled her to him so that they were joined more firmly together, she could feel the hard, unmistakable evidence of his own arousal, against her bare thigh.

His mouth was at her ear now, murmuring her name. 'Ah, Bianca, Bianca,' he breathed softly. 'You feel so good. I've wanted to hold you like this for so long. Put your arms around me, darling. Hold me. Love me.'

Her breath was coming in quick gasps now. The clean smell of his skin, the roughness of the short bristles on his chin, his strong arms holding her, were irresistible. And why should she resist? she asked herself dimly as she raised her arms and slid them up around his neck. It was what she wanted, what she realised now she had wanted from the day she first saw him standing so straight and tall and arrogant in the window of the house next door.

'Ah, that's the way,' he said when her hands began to move on the back of his neck, then under the loose collar of the shirt to his hard muscular back.

With both arms enfolding her, he kissed her again. Her fingers raked through the dark hair at the back of his head, thick, silky and vibrant. He opened his mouth slightly, and she felt the tip of his tongue run tentatively over her lips, moist and warm and inviting. When she responded by parting her own lips instead of drawing back in alarm, she heard a low growl deep in his throat and his arms tightened around her, moving his hands over her back from her shoulders to her waist.

This is Gerry, she thought to herself as she melted against him, and she knew that she, too, had been waiting for this moment as much as he had. The feel of his hard body all along the length of hers, the sweet taste of his mouth, the pungent smell of his skin, were all like coming home, reaching the one place she truly belonged after a long, lonely journey.

He tore his mouth away from hers and held her chin firmly in one hand, tilting her head back so that she was forced to look up into his eyes, alight with passion.

'Bianca,' he said hoarsely. 'You know how badly I want you.'

She nodded and swallowed convulsively. 'Yes,' she murmured.

The hand on her chin slid down to lightly grasp

her around the neck, the long fingers moving in a slow gentle rhythm until they reached the open collar of her cotton shirt. The light in his eyes grew brighter and a muscle along his jaw twitched as the hand then settled over her breast, resting there, the soft fullness fitting perfectly into the curved palm.

She couldn't move, could hardly breathe. She wanted to die right there. She hadn't known, hadn't dreamed she could feel like this, like a mindless vessel waiting to be filled. The only reality in the universe was the man holding her.

He dropped his glance lower, and she closed her eyes, sighing, as she felt his hand move across to her other breast, then slowly begin to unbutton her blouse.

'I want to look at you,' he muttered as his fingers worked deftly. When he reached the last button, he pushed aside the material and settled both his hands on her bare midriff, just below the filmy bra. Then they inched up slowly to cover her breasts.

She gasped when she felt his fingers graze gently over her nipples under the thin gauze, felt them harden and grow taut with burgeoning desire, felt his warm insistent mouth on the soft swell above the scant covering of her bra.

She began to tremble under the sensuous onslaught. She couldn't handle this. The feelings those clever fingers and mouth were evoking in her threatened to overwhelm her. She had no resistance. She knew with certainty that he could do whatever he wanted with her. She wanted it all, had no power to refuse him anything he asked from her.

His hands came up now to cup her face. 'What's wrong, darling?' she heard him ask. She opened her eyes. Her forehead was drawn in concern. He traced her trembling lips with one finger.

'I . . . I . . .' She couldn't seem to make her throat function properly. She wanted to tell him how much she loved him, desired him, but the words wouldn't come.

'God,' he breathed, enfolding her in his arms again. 'I've scared you to death.' His cheek was against hers, and he was murmuring in her ear. 'I'm so sorry, darling. I promise I'll never hurt you. I don't want to rush you into something you're not ready for. Just let me hold you. We've got lots of time.'

Bianca wanted to cry out to him, to tell him she was ready, she didn't want to wait, she wanted him to possess her now. The feel of his warm hard flesh against her bare stomach and half-uncovered breast was torture to her now, and only made her ache for more. But she knew he was right. It was too soon. She was not emotionally equipped to handle the overwhelming sensations he had aroused in her.

'Gerry,' she said at last against his rough cheek, 'I didn't realise it would be like this. It's just bowled me over.'

He put his hands on her shoulders and drew slightly away from her. He smiled, kissed her lightly on the tip of her nose and then reached down and slowly, reluctantly, began to rebutton her blouse.

'You're a witch, you know that?' he said playfully when he had finished and his hands were back on her shoulders again. 'I think you've become transformed into a real gypsy.' He shook his head slowly from side to side with a rueful air. 'The last thing I ever thought would happen to me was to fall in love.'

'Oh, Gerry,' she breathed happily.

With a sigh, he pulled her to him and held her tenderly, his mouth in her hair. She slid her arms around his waist and nestled comfortably against him. She wished she could just stay there forever in his arms, and she moved her hands up under his shirt, aching for the feel of his skin.

He drew back abruptly, and with his hands firmly clamped on her shoulders, held her a little distance away from him. The heavy-lidded eyes were still smouldering, but the jaw was firm, the set of his sensuous mouth determined. She gazed at him in bewilderment. Didn't he want her? Was she being too easy? She reddened. Her body went rigid and she started to pull farther away from him.

But he held her fast, and the grim expression in his face softened at her obvious distress. 'Did you think I was going to let you seduce me so soon?' he asked playfully.

She lowered her eyes. 'Gerry,' she began.

He put one finger under her chin and tilted it up so that she had to face him. 'Listen, you little fruitcake, this is no game I'm playing.' The corners of his mouth quirked up in a wry smile. 'Hell, I'm probably out of my mind not to take you to bed right now, but I want more than a quick roll in the hay with you, Bianca, more than a summer affair. I want a commitment, something beyond fun and games.' He frowned. 'Don't you, Bianca? Maybe I'm taking too much for granted. Maybe a girl like you couldn't possibly take a man like me seriously. You really don't know anything about me.'

This sudden burst of uncharacteristic humility, this apparent cracking of that arrogant self-assurance, his letting her see the chink in his armour, was all that it took to clear away any lingering doubts she had about his sincerity. A heady sense of her own power over this man came to her, and she reached out a hand and gently traced it along his finely chiselled mouth.

'I know all I need to know,' she said in a voice full of love. 'I know you're generous and kind and,' she grinned, 'that you are a very serious person.'

He grasped her wrist and brought the palm of her hand to his lips. 'You know,' he said evenly, his eyes never leaving hers, 'the time is going to come when I'm not going to want to stop, won't be able to stop. I'm going to have to make love to you properly. Violent, passionate love.'

'I know,' she said quietly.

'But not until you're ready.' He inhaled a deep breath. 'When that happens we can decide just what we want to do about it.'

She nodded her agreement, but in her heart she knew there wasn't the slightest doubt what she wanted to do about it. She wanted to spend the rest of her live with this wonderful man, to make a home for him, have his children. The intense, overpowering love she felt for him was light years beyond mere physical desire, as compelling as that was, even beyond her commitment to music.

But, she decided, she wouldn't tell him that just yet. She'd do it his way. He was right. She needed time to get her feelings under control. This was her first real experience with passionate love. They had lots of time.

She fluttered her eyelashes up at him. 'Of course, Gerry,' she said demurely. 'I think you're absolutely right.'

CHAPTER SEVEN

BIANCA floated through the next few weeks in a dream. It was May now. She'd been at the beach for almost four months and had never been happier. The pale depressed girl who had appeared in February had been transformed into a sun-browned, sparkling woman. She enjoyed her playing at Rumania House thoroughly now after those first difficult weeks, and found that it satisfied her artistic drive completely for now.

She was also falling more deeply in love with Gerry every day. By tacit agreement and sheer power of will, they had managed to keep their desire for each other within bounds. Both were long accustomed to self-discipline, and Bianca guessed that while much of her desire for Gerry was transmuted into the stirring gypsy music she played each evening at the restaurant, he probably put his own frustrated longing into his writing.

Their daily routine continued to follow the same pattern, but now he was far more open with her than he had been at first. She learned that he came from a small town in northern California, that Flicka was his only sister, that his father was dead, his mother living in Florida, and that he had attended the University of California at Berkeley for two years until his father died and he had to leave to go to work.

He was full of surprises. It seemed there wasn't anything he hadn't done. One Sunday evening before supper Bianca was sitting at the kitchen table leafing idly through an old vacation travel magazine while Gerry was getting steaks ready to put on the outdoor grill, when she came across some spectacular photographs of Glacier National Park in the Montana Rockies.

'Oh, look, Gerry,' she cried. 'Isn't this beautiful?' City-bred, she'd never seen such gorgeous scenery. 'Look at that lovely lake and the snow on the mountains.'

He peered over her shoulder on his way to the refrigerator, one hand resting lightly on the back of her neck as he bent over to look at the coloured photographs. He pointed at the picture of the lake. The snow-capped mountains plunged down steeply to its shores and a chalet-type lodge was at one end of it.

'That's Many Glacier Hotel,' he said. 'I used to work there in the summertime.' His fingers were working their way up through her short curly hair. 'We'll go there sometime if you like. It's really something. Lots of wildlife. Big-horn sheep, grizzly bears, brown bears, beavers, just about every species of native animal.'

She twisted around to gaze up at him. 'You worked there?' He nodded, grinning, his hand now gently massaging her back. 'What did you do?'

'Let's see. One summer I waited on tables in the dining room, another I was a bellhop. It was great. College kids from all over the country worked there. The hotel required some musical talent for employment, and we provided all the entertainment.'

'And that's where you played piano in the combo you told me about?'

He nodded again. 'Among other things, other

places. I even did a little cooking when I was at Glacier.'

She stared up at him. 'Is there anything you haven't done?' she asked, almost purring under the sensations the gentle strokes of his fingers were creating in her. The hand had come around now to the front of her neck, the slow motion almost hypnotising her.

He tilted his head and seemed to be giving her question serious consideration. 'Well,' he said at last, 'I've never been a brain surgeon or a bank robber.'

The hand had slipped down now inside her blouse to cover her breast and began to move lightly from one to the other. She closed her eyes and leaned her head back over the railing of the chair. His mouth came down on hers, then, and the hand on her breast tightened, cupping the fullness.

'I'd better get these steaks on,' he murmured against her lips. His mouth nipped at hers. He took her lower lip gently between his teeth and she felt his tongue glide back and forth over the sensitive skin. 'There's no telling where this will end if I don't.' Reluctantly, his hand slid back up to her cheek.

She opened her eyes and stared up at him. 'You look funny upside down,' she said with a nervous giggle.

'Oh, yeah?' he jeered. 'I'll show you funny!' His hand snaked down to her ribs and started to tickle her unmercifully until finally she had to beg him to stop.

Later that night, after he had gone back to the house next door and she was getting ready for bed, she found herself wishing so strongly that he had stayed with her, that for a moment she was tempted to call him and tell him to come back, or, better, go next door herself to surprise him. It was getting harder and harder to let him go each night, for him, too, she knew, and she wondered where it was all going to end. She had the feeling he was waiting for something before carrying their relationship on to the next logical step. But what was that step? He didn't want an affair, she was certain of that. Marriage? Was Gerry the kind of man who could settle down to one woman?

As she sat at the dressing table brushing her hair, she thought about the differences in their backgrounds. He had been on his own from the time he was nineteen and had a wide and varied experience of life. She had the feeling that no matter how forthcoming he was about his past, she still hadn't begun to discover all there was to know about him. There was a strangely elusive quality to Gerry, as though he was doling out information piecemeal, never revealing everything.

Well, she thought dreamily, as she settled into bed and turned out the light, I'll just have to trust him. Isn't that what love means? And she did love him. Of that she was certain. With her whole heart and soul she felt committed to him, and she had no doubt that he loved her. With that to bind them together, what could possibly go wrong?

The next night was a work night. Bianca had arrived at the restaurant and was sitting at the cluttered dressing table in her costume applying her stage make-up when Madame Tedescu burst into the tiny room calling her name in an agonised voice.

'Bianca, a disaster. A terrible thing.'

Bianca glanced up in alarm at their reflections in the mirror. The little woman was wringing her hands, her wrinkled face contorted. Bianca whirled around on the narrow bench. 'What is it? What's happened?' She had visions of a serious accident, a death in the family, an invasion from Mars.

Madame Tedescu groaned and flung her head back dramatically, one ring-encrusted hand pressed to her forehead. 'What has *not* happened?' she cried. 'The chef has cut himself boning chicken for the paprikash. Diane has sprained her ankle jogging.' The bright black eyes widened in horror. 'Jogging! Can you imagine anyone inflicting such torture on herself? As if that weren't enough,' she went on in a rush, 'Dino has called in sick. A virus!' She spat out the word with venom, as though it were a malediction from the gods.

Bianca relaxed and expelled the breath she had been holding all during the excited recitation. Really, the woman was so dramatic. She should be used to her theatrics by now.

'Well, now, Madame,' she soothed, 'it's not as bad as all that. It's only Tuesday night. We don't get a very big crowd during the week. Barbara and I can cover the music all right, but I'm afraid I can't help you in the kitchen. Can't someone else do the cooking?'

Bianca's matter-of-fact tone seemed to have a calming effect on the distraught woman. Heaving a dramatic sigh, she pulled herself up to her full five feet and placed her hand over her heart.

'*I* will do the cooking,' she announced. Her voice rang with renewed courage, as though she had just declared her intention of storming the Bastille singlehanded. Her sharp little eyes fastened on Bianca. 'You are sure you and Barbara can manage without Dino and Diane?'

Bianca shrugged. It would be a long night, and she would especially miss Dino. A good accompanist was a tremendous help in covering up little mistakes, especially towards the end of the evening when she was tired. She decided not to mention this to Madame Tedescu, however. It would only set her off again.

'Yes,' she replied finally in a reassuring tone. 'Don't worry.'

'Very well.' Madame pulled back her narrow shoulders and lifted her chin. 'I must get now to my kitchen.' With a brave little smile, she turned and swept out of the room.

When Barbara came, Bianca explained the situation to her. After she had finished, the two women looked at each other with some anxiety.

'We'll have to cut our breaks short,' Barbara said at last. Bianca nodded ruefully. She needed those breaks. Barbara sighed sadly. 'And I will miss Dino.' Bianca agreed. 'Let's just hope he gets well by tomorrow night.'

The evening wasn't as bad as they had anticipated. As Bianca had expected, the Tuesday night crowd was light and not so demanding on the two violinists as a weekend group would have been. Madame Tedescu's culinary efforts seemed to be well-received, and to all outward appearances the restaurant was running as smoothly as ever.

By eleven o'clock, however, Bianca felt dead on her feet. The two women had decided at the beginning of the evening that with only two of them playing, it would work best if each of them covered a separate half of the dining room, rather than wandering aimlessly as they usually did. They also decided that they'd take their shortened supper break together, on the basis that it was better to have no music at all than only one player trying to cover the whole area.

By eleven there were still several late diners seated at the tables in the various sections and the requests for favourite tunes kept coming. Bianca had just finished playing a request when Barbara approached her side, a worried frown on her normally placid face.

'What's up?' Bianca asked in a low voice.

'Trouble, I'm afraid.'

Bianca groaned. 'That's all we need. What is it?'

Barbara motioned with her head back in the direction of her own section. 'There's some guy down there who keeps asking for a song I don't even know.' She pursed her lips. 'I've been avoiding him, but he's getting insistent—and loud—and drunk. I wish Dino was here.'

'Which one is he?' Bianca asked, craning her neck to get a better view.

'That bald guy with the cigar sitting alone back in the first section. You can probably hear him.'

Bianca glanced past Barbara and saw a heavyset man waving a cigar in the air and singing offkey. 'What song does he want?' she asked anxiously.

Barbara gave her a guilty look. *"When A Gypsy Makes His Violin Cry,'* she replied. 'You play it so often that I just never bothered to learn it,' she went on defensively.

Bianca sighed. 'Oh, all right. You take over here, and I'll go see if I can keep him quiet. It's almost closing time anyway.'

Wearily, Bianca made her way down to the far end of the long room. She stepped inside the lattice-enclosed dining section and, taking a deep breath, started walking towards the table where the man was now singing loudly. There were five other tables in the area, all of them occupied, she noticed with an inward groan of dismay, and all of the other diners' eyes seemed to be firmly fastened on the drunken man.

'Sir,' she said, smiling down at him. 'I understand you have a request.'

The man closed his mouth abruptly, shutting off the flow of sound, and turned his bleary gaze on her. He nodded happily. '*When A Gypsy Makes His Violin Cry*,' he slurred, trying hard to enunciate each word clearly and failing dismally.

Bianca smiled again and lifted her bow. He seems harmless, she thought, as she began to play the sobbing melody. Certainly not dangerous or threatening. Perhaps the music would soothe him. As she played, she glanced down at him from time to time and noticed that tears were rolling down his cheeks as he hummed along with her offkey. She also noticed that his musical efforts were interspersed with long swallows from the amber-coloured glass in his hands.

'Beautiful!' he cried out, applauding noisily, when she had finished. He reached into his wallet, pulled out a bill and held it up to her. 'Beautiful,' he repeated soulfully.

Bianca took the bill from him and, as usual, slipped it into the bodice of her dress. With another smile and a nod, she thanked him and began to move away, congratulating herself on having handled a sticky situation rather well.

Then she felt his hand on her arm, quite a firm grip, she realised as she tried to pull free. Apprehensive now, she turned to face him again.

'Play it again,' he demanded thickly.

'I'm sorry, sir,' she began to explain, 'but we're short-handed tonight and . . .'

'I gave you ten dollars,' he broke in, giving her a sullen look. He pointed accusingly at the bosom of her dress with his free hand. 'That should pay for an encore.'

Bianca didn't know what to do. He had a point. What she *wanted* to do was just get away from the clutching man any way she could. If she stayed and played for him again, he might never let her escape. If she freed herself by force, he might get really ugly. One glance at his petulant frown told her he was already showing signs of it.

Finally, she decided to go with her feelings. She reached down and began to pry his fingers off her arm. 'I'm really very sorry, sir,' she said in as calm and soothing a tone as she could muster in her growing distress. 'I really have to move on. I'll be happy to return your money if you . . .'

Suddenly, he was on his feet. The table came crashing down in front of him. He lunged at her, one hand tightening his grip on her arm, the other clawing at the bodice of her dress.

'You bet you'll give me back my money, you little bitch!' he was shouting.

Before Bianca could even react to this sudden attack, she saw the man rise up in the air and give a howl of pain. She stared, wide-eyed, and saw a tall blond man with a heavy moustache holding her tormentor by the scruff of his neck two feet off the ground, then slam him down hard in the chair, where he sat moaning and holding his head.

It was all happening so fast that Bianca was left speechless, breathless, almost in a state of shock. She had noticed the tall man earlier when she had first arrived and scanned the other diners, but he had been sitting alone in a dim corner, and she had been concentrating so hard on placating the drunk that she hadn't paid any attention to the others in the room.

Now, watching the tall man as he set the table back on its legs and shoved it hard against the still moaning drunk in the chair, she felt that something about him seemed vaguely familiar. When he turned to look her full in the face, she knew.

'Gerry!' she breathed. 'What . . .'

Then, steely-eyed and grim, he grasped her roughly by the shoulders. 'We're getting out of here,' he ground out angrily. 'Go get your things.'

She continued to stare at him, open-mouthed. That hair! That moustache! And what was he doing here? Then she knew. He had tricked her, disguised himself so she wouldn't recognise him, knowing she didn't want him here.

'Go!' he repeated in a threatening tone. He was looming over her now, and the tight grip bit painfully into her shoulders.

'No,' she said, growing angry now herself. What right did he have to come barging in here ordering her around? He wasn't even supposed to be here.

'No?' he repeated, his voice dangerously soft, a menacing gleam in the black eyes.

He picked her up, flung her over one broad shoulder and stalked out of the dining room, into the foyer and out on to the street. She began beating on his back with one fist, her violin and bow clutched in the other hand, but she might as well have been pounding against a granite wall.

She felt the fake hairpiece come off her head and fall to the pavement as he marched towards the parking lot in long purposeful strides. Her dress was torn where the drunk had pulled at it, and she watched in horror as her money fell out of the bodice and floated away.

'Put me down, you animal!' she cried, still pounding feebly on his back. 'My hair! My money!'

They had arrived at a sleek, dark, low-slung car by now. Gerry opened the passenger door and dumped her unceremoniously inside. She was so concerned about protecting her priceless violin and bow that before she could make a move, he was in the driver's seat beside her, the engine started, and driving like a maniac, with tyres squealing, out on to the boulevard.

She was so angry by this time she was trembling. She turned to glare at him. He was driving more carefully now out in the traffic of the main thoroughfare, and had pulled off the fake moustache and blond wig. His jaw was set, his mouth clamped in a hard angry line. When she saw the thunderous expression on his face, the stinging accusation she was about to deliver died on her lips.

Why was he angry with her? For a moment fear clutched at her heart. The distance between them on the front seat of the car was only a few inches, but it might have been a hundred miles, and she felt bereft at the way he was shutting her out so coldly.

Then she began to feel her own anger return. What did she have to feel guilty about? *He* was the one who had broken his word and come to the restaurant in that stupid disguise. *He* was the one who had humiliated her in front of a roomful of interested spectators, made her lose all her tips and almost ruined her violin. And her car and clothes were still back at the restaurant, she suddenly remembered with a sinking feeling.

She crossed her arms firmly across her chest, and gave him a withering look. 'Turn this car around right now, Gerry,' she demanded in what she hoped was a firm, no-nonsense tone.

'Shut up,' he snarled, and shot her a brief glance of such contempt and fury that she instinctively shrank away from him.

'I don't know who you think you are . . .' she tried again.

This time he shouted. 'I said shut up!'

They were stopped at a busy, well-lighted intersection, and when she got a clearer view of that forbidding countenance, she decided she'd better do as he said for now. He seemed to be keeping himself barely under control with an almost heroic effort. The cords along his neck were bulging, the knuckles of his hands gripping the steering wheel were white, and she could hear his laboured breathing over the noise of the car engine and nearby traffic.

She decided to sulk. She didn't think he'd actually hurt her, but she was certain he wanted to. She flounced over to the far edge of the seat, pressing herself up against the car door, and gazed stonily out the window.

When they reached the beach house, he stopped the car, pulled viciously at the emergency brake and before Bianca could collect her violin and bow, he had moved swiftly out of the car, around in front and was pulling her door open.

'Get out,' he ordered, in a gritty tone.

'I was just going to,' she muttered, and with as much dignity as she could summon up, she got out of the car, clutching the instrument in one hand

and holding her torn bodice together with the other.

She sailed past him with her head in the air, and it wasn't until she had taken several steps that it dawned on her this was not Laura's house. She whirled around to face him. He was just a few paces behind her. He stopped short and stood with his long legs apart, his fists resting on his hips.

He made a jerking motion forward with his head. 'Go on.' He didn't sound quite so angry now.

'I'm not going in there,' she stated flatly.

'Yes you are.' His hooded dark eyes flashed a warning at her. 'If I have to carry you again.'

He'd do it, too, she knew now from experience. With a little sniff of disdain, she turned and started walking again towards the entrance of the house, which she now recognised as the one next door where Gerry was staying. She couldn't get into Laura's house anyway, she thought philosophically, since her keys were in the handbag she had left behind at Rumania House.

At the door, Gerry stepped in front of her to unlock it, then flicked on a light and stood aside while she stepped over the threshold. He closed the door behind him and strode past her into a large sunken living room. The far wall was one vast expanse of glass, and with a little jolt, Bianca recalled the day she had seen him standing at that very window. He was standing there now, his back to her, his arms folded in front of him, gazing out into the dark night.

Suddenly, all the anger left her. Not only was she exhausted from the gruelling evening of playing and emotionally drained from the encounter with the drunk, but it tore her apart to see

Gerry so cold to her, so tight and distant, so angry. He had behaved badly tonight, but even though he shouldn't have been in the restaurant at all, she couldn't help but be grateful to him for rescuing her from what had been developing into a really ugly scene.

She set her violin and bow down on a table near the door and began to walk slowly towards him over the thick plush carpet. He didn't move until she was directly behind him. She put out a hand to touch him tentatively on his rigid back. Then he flinched. She could feel the tense, hard muscle recoiling under her fingers, see it ripple under the thin white shirt.

'Gerry,' she said softly.

He whirled around, then, wild-eyed, and his fingers bit into her shoulders. She stared up into those fathomless black pools and winced at the pain she saw there.

'Bianca,' he choked out. 'I'm so sorry. I know I behaved like a maniac, but you can't imagine what it did to me to see you there tonight—*my* Bianca—in that awful costume . . .' He broke off and turned his head away, his hands kneading her shoulders painfully.

'Gerry, that's why I didn't want you to come. Don't you understand?' she pleaded. 'That's not me. That's only a performer. It's only a disguise. It's the music that's important.'

'God, Bianca,' he muttered, 'when I saw that guy pawing at you, I was so close to murdering him—or you . . .'

He turned back to her. His face was still pale under his tan, but more relaxed now, and he was even making a feeble effort to smile. Shyly, she raised her hand and placed it on his lips, tracing the outline of the beautiful mouth with trembling fingers.

'I'm still your Bianca, Gerry,' she crooned. 'I love you.'

With a groan he gathered her into his arms, murmuring her name over and over again in her ear, on her forehead, her eyes, until finally his mouth came down to cover hers. There was no gentleness in him now, no playfulness, only an aching, driving need. The hard body trembled against hers, and through the thin material of the ruined costume, she could feel the strength and extent of his pulsing arousal.

Her mouth parted joyfully under his, and immediately his thrusting tongue was inside, probing deeply into every crevice. She put her arms around his neck and gave herself up totally to the warm sensuous mouth. The large hands moved feverishly now over her slight body, first spanning her waist, then running up along her fragile ribs, brushing against the sides of her breasts, then sliding back down to clutch at her hips and pull her lower body hungrily against his where his grinding need raised her to an even higher pitch of desire.

Her own fingers slipped under the collar of his shirt, then came around and moved down to his waist. She pulled the shirt out of his trousers and ran her hands underneath it and up over the smooth chest, the muscles and skin quivering at her touch.

She sensed dimly that they had crossed over into a new territory of sensuality, had passed a point from which there was no return. His demand and her response were total this time, with no holding back. She gave herself up to the rapture of the moment, her blood singing in her veins, her heart yearning, her mind empty of everything except the exciting man in her arms.

He tore his mouth from hers and jerked his head up. The dark gaze fastened intently on her. 'I want you, Bianca,' he choked out hoarsely. 'I want you now.'

There was a question in the hard statement, she knew, and for answer she reached up and placed both palms flat against his rough lean cheeks. She smiled at him, her eyes glowing with answering passion.

'Yes,' she whispered. 'Oh, yes.'

A muscle twitched by his mouth. He closed his eyes for a moment, then opened them again and reached out for her. His hands were heavy on her shoulders, the thumbs caressing the base of her neck. Then, his eyes never leaving hers, he very slowly slid his hands down until they came to rest on her high firm breasts, half-exposed under the torn dress.

She closed her eyes. With a sigh, she let her head fall backward a little, giving herself up to the fiery sensations that coursed through her body. His fingers trailed first along the smooth fullness above the ragged hem of the bodice, then moved to fondle the taut peaks with a rhythmic circular motion that sent a shaft of fire directly to the centre of her desire.

He brushed the torn edges of the bodice apart and slid the dress off her shoulders, down her arms and along her hips until it slid with a slight swishing sound to settle at her feet. His hands were back at her waistline now, tugging at the sheer tights, pulling them down off her hips and along her legs, then lifting each foot to release them.

Finally, she stood naked before him. She felt his hands grasp her ankles, then glide slowly up her calves, her thighs. He was kneeling before her, his moist mouth following the magic feathery fingers up over her legs to her flat stomach.

She reached down and raked her fingers through the silky strands of his smooth dark hair, drowning in the sensations aroused by his hands and mouth. Then she felt him raise himself up in one quick movement. She watched him tear off his shirt and slip swiftly out of his trousers, and then they were clinging together again with not a shred of clothing separating them at last.

He picked her up in his arms and with her head against his shoulder, her mouth on his neck, carried her off down a long hallway. He kicked open a door and laid her gently on top of a bed, easing himself down beside her, one hair-roughened leg flung over hers. He propped himself up on his elbows and gazed down into her eyes.

'I love you, Bianca. You know that, don't you?'

She nodded happily. 'I know, Gerry. And I love you.'

He kissed her then, a long sweet kiss, his open mouth pulling at her lips as though to draw out her very soul. A deep ache began to pierce her loins, a longing to have all of him, to possess him completely.

'Trust me, darling,' he murmured as his mouth left hers and travelled downward.

When she felt his lips enclose the peak of one breast, she gasped in sheer delight. His tongue worked its magic on the hardening nipple, while his hand moved langourously over her other breast, then down along her hips, her thighs, to settle between her legs.

When she could bear no more of the sweet torment, she cried out his name. He came up to cover her writhing body with his own, and at last, after one brief sharp stab of pain, they were joined together completely in a union that carried her gradually to the pinnacle of ecstasy, over the edge, and with a burst of exquisite sensation, tumbled her shuddering over to the other side.

Finally spent, he collapsed against her with a groan of fulfilment. He lay on top of her for several moments as his harsh breathing quieted down. She could feel his pounding heart against her breast settle into a steadier, gentler rhythm, and she kissed the cheek that lay on the pillow next to her own.

'Gerry,' she whispered. 'That was beautiful.'

With a groan, he rolled off her and held her close. 'Did I hurt you, darling?' he murmured in her ear.

'Not really. I'm so glad and grateful that you were the first. You're a wonderful teacher.'

His hold on her tightened. 'That's because I love you so much,' he mumbled sleepily.

She felt his eyelashes flutter against her cheek. His hands relaxed, and she heard the steady even breathing that told her he was asleep. She curled herself into the contours of his body and closed her eyes.

CHAPTER EIGHT

THE instant Bianca awoke the next morning, she was immediately aware of the hard masculine body lying next to her and the smooth bare flesh under her hand. The memory of last night's lovemaking was still fresh in her mind, and with an apparent will of its own, her hand started moving downward over a flat stomach until another stronger hand clutched hers firmly and held it in place.

'You'd better not start something unless you're going to finish it,' came a deep husky voice.

She opened her eyes. Gerry was propped up against a pillow, his broad chest and shoulders bare, the black hair tousled over his forehead. For a moment she could only stare up into the warm dark eyes, then, feeling suddenly shy, she tensed, pulled her hand away and turned her head towards the window, where the morning sunshine was streaming through.

His arms came around her from behind then, pulling her up against him. 'Hey, I wasn't objecting,' came his low voice in her ear.

She felt the warm breath in her hair, on her cheek, and she relaxed back into the body curved around her own. They lay there quite still for several moments, their hearts beating as one. His hands were resting possessively on her breasts and without moving her head, she glanced down at them. Something about the sight of those large brown hands curled around the white flesh made her catch her breath in a near sob of joy.

As though attuned to every nuance of her inner thoughts and feelings, his breath became more shallow, the heartbeat against her back quickened, and she watched, entranced, as the long tapering fingers began to move on her breast in a slow, gentle kneading rhythm. A delicious warmth began to steal through her, and her own pulse started to race as one hand moved downward.

Then, suddenly, he took a deep breath and turned her around to face him, her body limp and pliable in his arms. He moved away from her, pulled the sheet up to cover her and tucked it firmly under her arms. He propped himself up on one elbow and touched her lightly on the nose.

'Before we start that,' he said firmly, easing his long body farther away from her, 'we've got to talk.'

Bianca tensed at his cool withdrawal. She was suddenly afraid of what was coming. She hadn't pleased him. She was too inexperienced for a man like Gerry. He was going to tell her he didn't want her. But he'd said he loved her, she thought wildly. In today's parlance, though, what did that mean? To her, it meant commitment, total and irrevocable. To a man like Gerry it could mean anything from a one-night stand to . . . To what? What was the extent of his conception of involvement?

She steeled herself to look calmly into his eyes. 'Yes,' she replied in a steady voice. 'I'm ready.'

He leaned back on the propped-up pillow, his arms behind his head. He was frowning slightly, as though deep in thought. She longed to run her fingers over his forehead, down the straight strong nose, the fine sensuous mouth, the firm jaw and chin, covered now with a fine dark stubble. But she waited, afraid to move, even to breathe.

'Well, as I see it,' he went on in a remote, businesslike tone, 'the first issue we've got to settle is how soon we can get married. In California, it takes three days to . . .'

'Married!' she cried. It was the last thing she had expected him to say.

He gave her a puzzled look. 'Certainly, married. What did you think, that I made a hobby of going around seducing virgins just for the fun of it?' There was a hurt tone to his voice. He gazed grimly at her, a sudden flicker gleaming in the hooded black eyes. 'Bianca, don't you want to marry me?'

She flung herself on him with a sob of joy. 'Of course I want to marry you,' she cried into his chest. She lifted her head to gaze up at him. 'I just thought . . .'

He placed a finger under her chin. 'What did you think, Bianca?'

She reddened and lowered her eyes. 'I wasn't thinking, I guess.' She gave him a pleading look. 'This is all so new to me, Gerry. I'm out of my depth. I wasn't sure what you expected, what you wanted.'

'Bianca, I *love* you,' he said earnestly. 'You're the most wonderful thing that's ever happened to me. I admit my life hasn't always been strictly conventional. I've done things, seen things, had experiences that I'm not proud of. But I told you from the beginning that I wanted to put all that behind me.' He reached for her and pulled her up into his arms, burying his dark head in her neck. 'I can't do that without you, Bianca,' he said in a muffled voice.

She stroked his hair and kissed his face. He loves me, her heart sang, and he wants to marry me, spend his life with me. She had never conceived such joy was possible. As she cradled his head in her arms, drawing it now down to her breast, she murmured her love for him in a low crooning voice. She felt fiercely protective of this strong man who had made himself so vulnerable to her, who had literally placed his heart, his life, his happiness in her hands.

She felt his fingers moving now in long sweeping strokes along her thigh, her hip, her waist and up to her breasts. Cupping them from the sides, he buried his mouth in the valley between them, then covered each soft, milky mound with hot, languorous kisses, until she felt her bones grow weak. Her breath was coming now in short panting gasps. He rolled on to his back and pulled her on top of him, his hands firmly pressing her lower body against his hard strong arousal.

This time there was no twinge of pain and none of the urgency of last night's experience. With slow, deep, steady movements, he brought her once again to the peak of fulfilment. As they climbed the mountain together and then went over the edge at the same instant, their hoarse mingled cries of ecstatic union filled the silent room.

After a late leisurely breakfast together, Gerry left her and drove down to Rumania House to retrieve her coat and handbag. When he returned, he took her back to Laura's house so that she could shower and change her clothes.

'Need any help?' she heard him call to her as she luxuriated under the warm spray in the stall shower.

The deep voice startled her. She'd never had a man in the bathroom with her before. Recovering herself, she smiled. 'Yes,' she called back. 'The living room needs vacuuming, and you might see what you can do about mending my costume.'

The glass door was suddenly wrenched open, and he was standing there with a wicked gleam in his eyes. 'Think you're pretty clever, don't you?' he said, cocking an eyebrow at her, and began pulling off his shirt.

She stood immobile under the spray and watched as he took off his shoes and socks, undid his belt buckle, unzipped his trousers and slid them down over his hips. When he was naked, he gave her another devilish grin, but in a second the smile faded, the eyelids came down halfway, and the playful look became one of raw hunger.

Then he was standing behind her, the shower door shut, his hands everywhere. He took the soap and lathered every inch of her body while she leaned back limply against him. His soap-slickened hands did magical thing to her senses, and finally, unable to bear another moment of the sweet torture, she turned into his arms and they clung together under the spray, their slippery bodies sliding against each other, their mouths locked.

They spent the rest of the afternoon talking, seated across from each other at the kitchen table so that they wouldn't be tempted to touch. Bianca was in a daze, thrilled to her very core to belong to this wonderful man who seemed to want only to be with her, to make her happy, to fill her with himself. His love for her seemed so direct, so simple, and absolutely unconditional.

'I think three,' he was saying thoughtfully now. 'Maybe four, if you feel up to it.'

'What in the world are you talking about?' she asked with a smile.

'Children, of course. Not for a while, yet. You're just a kid yourself.'

'I beg your pardon,' she retorted. 'I don't feel in the least like a kid, even if you did think I was a boy the first time we met.' Her voice softened. 'Whatever I was then, I'm a woman now.'

'All woman,' he murmured appreciatively. He reached across the table for her hand and laced his fingers through hers. 'And all mine.' He raised her hand to his mouth and pressed his lips against the palm. Then, carefully, he slid it back across the table and released it. 'That's not going to help,' he said huskily. 'We really do have to talk.'

She cleared her throat. 'Do you really want to get married in three days?'

'Unless you can think of a way of doing it sooner,' he rejoined immediately. 'I'm not going to let you go. I don't want to take any chances or waste a minute.'

'I wonder where we should live,' she mused dreamily. Living with Gerry, she thought happily. It seemed too good to be true. 'We can stay here until Laura comes back. When do your friends get back from Japan?'

'Not for another month.' He frowned. 'I suppose we're committed to taking care of both houses until they get back, so it really doesn't matter which one we live in. But I want us to get our own place as soon as possible. I want *our* home. I want to put down roots, build a solid life together, raise a family.'

There was one subject they hadn't discussed,

and it worried her. 'Gerry,' she said hesitantly, 'all these plans, all the things you want to do. Won't it cost a lot of money? My parents might be able to help us, but . . .'

He waved a hand in the air. 'Money's no problem,' he said shortly. 'Don't give it a thought.'

She wanted to ask him where the money was coming from, but something in the way he dismissed the subject warned her not to press the issue. She thought about the way he lived without working, the expensive car, his mother's luxury condo in Florida. Perhaps he'd had a large advance on his book, she thought, but somehow that didn't seem likely. It was a good book, but she didn't think a first novel would earn that kind of money, especially before it was even published.

At five o'clock he drove her to Rumania House so she could get ready to play that night. The red costume was beyond repair, and she needed to get there early enough to try on a new one from the rack in the dressing room. Gerry didn't want her to go back at all after last night's disturbance, but she insisted. With both Diane and Dino out of commission, she couldn't let Madame Tedescu down.

He dropped her off at the restaurant. She would have Laura's car to drive home in, and she still didn't want him to watch her playing in her costume and make-up, in spite of their new relationship, and over his vehement protests.

When she got home, well after midnight, Gerry was waiting for her. He spent the night in her bed, a night of slow, gentle lovemaking. At this point the legal formality of a marriage seemed redundant. They were so totally committed to each other, mind, body and soul, that a piece of paper hardly made a difference now.

He left right after breakfast the next morning. She wanted to make some telephone calls to her froends and family to tell them the news of her impending marriage, and she wanted to do it alone, without Gerry's disturbing presence. They had decided to ask Flicka and Tom to stand up for them at the wedding, and she needed to get hold of him as soon as possible.

Since she wanted to shop for a new dress for her wedding and Gerry was anxious to finish up the revision on his book, they decided to drive into town in separate cars and would meet at the county courthouse in Los Angeles at two o'clock that afternoon to get the licence and arrange for their blood tests. It was all happening so fast that she breathed a sigh of relief when he finally, reluctantly, left her to go next door. Somehow, she thought, telling her family and friends about it would make it more real. In the months she and Gerry had known each other they had lived virtually in a world of their own, isolated from their former lives, almost in a little cocoon. It was time to emerge into reality, she thought firmly, and telling people about him and their plans would be the first step.

But every number she tried was either busy or the person was unavailable. She wasn't even sure how to reach her parents, and was hoping Tom could help her, but when she finally got through to his office at UCLA, she was told that he was teaching a class. She left a message and asked that he call her back when he was free. The overseas call to Laura would have to wait until evening because of the time difference.

By ten o'clock she gave up. It was getting late. If she was to meet Gerry at two, she'd better get moving. The calls would have to wait.

She had never driven into Los Angeles by herself, but the city was laid out in a simple straightforward pattern of direct routes without the confusing triangular intersections so common in other cities. With the wonderful freeway system and the help of a map, she had no trouble finding her way, and in the middle of the morning the traffic was light.

She parked in a public lot and started down Broadway looking for a likely department store or dress shop where she might find a suitable wedding dress. The buildings were not nearly so tall here as they were in New York, and the streets were much wider, but the pavements seemed to be just as crowded with people.

Bianca enjoyed exploring new cities. It was a pleasant day, warm, smogless, and she wandered aimlessly around the city centre past the small shops, department stores, restaurants and cinemas. The courthouse wasn't far, and she headed up Hope Street in that direction to gauge her distance. It was still early, but she didn't want to be late for her appointment with Gerry.

There were several likely looking dress shops to choose from, and she had just about decided to go into the local branch of a large exclusive chain she was familiar with, when her eye was caught by a long line of people on the next block. Curious, she wandered past the shop to see what was going on.

When she reached the intersection, she could see that the line curved clear around the corner, and that its objective was a cinema. Imagine, she thought, going to the movies in the morning! It must be something really special to attract such a crowd at this hour.

She glanced up at the marquee, a white background bordered in blinking neon lights that seemed somehow garishly inappropriate in broad daylight. There were bold black letters on the marquee, and as she idly spelled them out, it took a moment for it to register. She blinked and read them again. 'Gerald Richards Festival' the letters said, and down below, 'Sex Symbol of the Seventies'.

No, she thought, swaying slightly in the bright sunshine as it hit her. It couldn't be. The name was a coincidence. Then she vaguely recalled that he had said something once about having done some acting. The light changed. People began to flow past her across the street. In a daze, she stumbled after them, drawn by an overwhelming, irresistible force. She had to find out.

At the front of the cinema was a large placard with a life-sized photographic cut-out of a half-naked man. When she was still several feet away from it, Bianca knew it was Gerry. She stood in front of it now, staring, still unable to take it all in.

His face in the photograph looked a little younger than he did now, but there was no mistaking the arrogant lift to his chin, the same hooded black eyes. The beautiful mouth she knew so well smiled seductively with the hint of a sensuous promise. The wide-muscled shoulders and smooth chest were bare, and he had on a brief pair of dark shorts. The image flashed into her mind once again of the day she had first seen him standing in the window of the house next door.

The long legs were spread apart, pelvis jutting forward slightly in a provocative stance, his fists resting on his narrow hips in the typical pose that was so familiar to her.

She felt suddenly sick and faint. Her throat was dry, her heart pounding madly, and for a moment a blank darkness threatened to swamp her and carry her into a blessed oblivion. Then her head cleared, and a new sensation began to flow through her, a sensation she recognised as anger and which was steadily building to a cold hard fury that was absolutely foreign to her experience.

The line of people was slowly moving now. Still in a daze, but with this overwhelming sense of outrage to sustain her, she marched purposefully to the ticket office, bought a ticket and moved to stand woodenly at the back of the line. All she knew was that she had to see this for herself.

As the line inched slowly forward, she distracted herself from the turmoil of her thoughts by listening to the conversations around her. The line seemed to be made up primarily of young girls, dressed in every conceivable outfit, from shabby jeans to miniskirts, and their comments to each other were delivered in short breathless gasps of anticipation.

'Honestly, Kathy,' a girl in front of her was saying to her companion, 'he is the sexiest thing I've ever seen. I just *drool* every time he gives the heroine that look.'

'I saw *Manhattan Madness* four times,' Kathy replied throatily. 'What a hunk!'

'That mouth!'

'That body!' The girl leaned over to whisper something in her friend's ear, and they both started to giggle.

Bianca's face and body burned with humiliation

and shame. They were talking about Gerry. Gerry! Discussing his anatomy down to the most minute detail, explicitly describing the way he kissed, made love, even took a shower! It couldn't be! Not her Gerry.

There was another conversation going on behind her. Bianca wanted to put her hands over her ears and scream, but she listened anyway. It was better than facing her own thoughts.

'I wish he'd make another movie,' a middle-aged woman was saying.

'Yes, it's been—how long—must be almost ten years.'

'And he only made four of them.'

The woman laughed. 'He probably made enough out of those to keep him in style the rest of his life.'

Finally, Bianca found herself inside the crowded cinema, sitting in the back row, one of the last to be admitted. The others would probably wait out there until the next show, she thought grimly as she sat rigidly in her seat. The lights dimmed, blessed darkness descended, and Bianca prepared herself for the worst as the large screen flickered into life.

It turned out to be far worse than she could possibly have anticipated, especially in view of her inexperience with the explicit nature of modern films. She sat virtually motionless through the two movies, stunned and sickened at what she saw. The whole experience was made a hundred times worse because of the magnification of the images on the screen.

In the close-ups, she could clearly see every beloved feature, even the faint stubble on his jaw and upper lip, the little dark mole on one thigh, the muscles rippling under the smooth skin as he embraced his leading lady or slowly undressed. Horrified, she watched him as he made love to the actress exactly as he had to her, never quite naked, but very near. It wasn't just the way he kissed her, open-mouthed, hungrily, or stroked the near-nude body. That was bad enough. But even worse were the little things, the way he smoothed the long blonde hair away from her forehead, or touched the pert nose with that familiar devilish grin on his face, the way he told her he wanted her, loved her, in the husky deep voice Bianca knew so well.

When it was over, she moved rigidly along with the crowd back out into the busy street. She blinked a little at the blinding sunshine, then marched determinedly across the street and past the store where she had intended to buy her wedding dress. Her wedding dress! What a joke!

She went directly to the car, got in and headed back to the beach. She felt soiled, dirty, and wanted to get as far away from that cinema as possible. Dry-eyed, with her teeth gritted together and her hands clamped on the wheel, her brain finally began to function.

It was all lies. The whole relationship was a lie. He was no better than a prostitute. That's where all the money had come from, she suddenly realised. He had sold that beautiful body, that handsome face as surely as any eager starlet on the casting couch. She shuddered in disgust now at the remembrance of his touch on her skin, his mouth on hers. She felt used, betrayed, her deepest affections poisoned. She remembered now the practised gestures and calculated poses that had struck her as being so artificial when she first met him. Why hadn't he told her? she agonised. Of course, she knew why. He was clever enough to realise that she would react in exactly the way she had. Still, he should have told her, at least prepared her. It was cruel to find out this way, and even if she could forgive him for what he had done in the past, she hated him for deceiving her.

By the time she arrived back at Laura's house she was shaking so badly that she was afraid she wouldn't be able to walk from the car to the house. Her one fear was that she would have to confront Gerry before she could get her things together and get far away. She glanced at her watch. It was a little past one o'clock. He wouldn't start calling her for another hour at least, when she didn't show up at the courthouse. Plenty of time, but she'd have to move fast.

She went straight to her bedroom, pulled down a suitcase from the wardrobe shelf and began to throw in the bare necessities. Her mind was working now with cold efficiency, her one aim to get out of California and back home as fast as possible. She called the airport and made a reservation on the late afternoon flight to New York. She would arrange later for Tom to pick up Laura's car and take care of Midnight for her.

When she had finished packing, she moved swiftly from room to room, checking taps, closing windows, straightening up as best she could. Mechanically, she stripped the bed she and Gerry had slept in last night, almost physically ill at the sight of it. It seemed she could still smell his masculine fragrance there, still see the indentation of his head on the pillow.

On her way to the laundry room with the sheets, she heard the doorbell ring. She stopped short. It was not quite two. It couldn't be Gerry. He was at the courthouse by now. Besides, he always came to the back door,. She decided to answer it in the hope it might be Tom responding to her call that morning. Her plane left at four. Maybe he could take her to the airport and she wouldn't have to leave Laura's car there.

She set the sheets down, ran to the front door and opened it. Gerry was standing there, a worried frown on his face. She was so surprised to see him that for one split second she could only stare.

'Bianca,' he said, 'what's wrong? I was driving by on my way downtown to meet you and I saw your car . . .'

Then, instinctively, she started to slam the door shut in his face. She couldn't bear the sight of him. But he was too quick for her, and had reached out swiftly to hold the door open. She pushed frantically on it, but he was too strong for her. For a moment, they simply stood there staring at each other, his expression stunned under her furious glare.

'Bianca . . .' he began again.

'Get out!' she spat at him. 'Get out of my house! Get out of my life!'

Still, he held the door open. His face was ashen, all the colour drained out of it, his lips tight and pinched. A pulse throbbed violently at his temple as he struggled to grasp what was going on. Then, with a mighty shove, he pushed the door open all the way, nearly knocking her off-balance, and stepped inside.

He closed the door behind him and leaned back against it, his eyes downcast, his mouth trembling, his shoulders slumped. She stood facing him holding her arms rigid at her sides with her hands balled into white-knuckled fists. The silence between them was electric. Her one thought was to get him out of here.

Finally, with a sigh, he raised his head and gave her a long look, his dark eyes filled with pain. 'You know,' he said quietly.

'Yes. I know,' she ground out.

'How did you find out?'

'What difference does it make? I saw you, that's all that matters.' She narrowed her eyes at him and her voice rose almost out of control. 'I *saw* you, Gerry, up on the silver screen, larger than life.' She laughed hysterically. 'The great lover himself. I see now where you learned all those clever tricks you used on me.'

'Bianca,' he groaned, 'don't. Please don't. That was a long time ago. I love you. I want to marry you.'

'Marry you!' she shouted. She knew her fury was reaching the limits of control, but she couldn't stop herself. He had wounded her to her very soul, cheapened beyond repair what had been between them, and all she wanted now was to lash out at him, to hurt him as deeply as he had hurt her.

He took a step towards her, and she shrank back from him. 'Don't come near me. Don't touch me. I don't ever want to see you or hear from you again. You're—you're nothing but a prostitute.'

His head snapped back at that, as though she had struck him. His eyes narrowed menacingly and he raised a hand in the air as if to ward off the dreadful accusation. She gazed with satisfaction at him and folded her arms in front of her, a look of scathing contempt on her face.

'Now, will you go?' she bit out.

He looked at her. 'You won't even let me explain?' he said quietly.

'Gerry, I *saw* everything. I spent the morning at the great Gerald Richards Festival.' She laughed hollowly. '"The Sex Symbol of the Seventies", that's you.' Her eyes narrowed. 'You've made a mockery of everything that was between us, made it cheap and dirty. I don't ever want to see you again. Just the sight of you sickens me and reminds me of my own stupid gullibility.'

'All right, Bianca,' he said at last. 'I can see there's no point in trying to reach you now. But you're wrong, you know. That's all in the past. It's over, has been for years.' The look in the dark eyes intensified. 'What happened between us wasn't cheap, wasn't dirty. It was real. It was beautiful. In time you'll forget . . .'

'I'll never, never forget,' she said in a dead, even tone of absolute finality. 'Now, will you please just go.'

'All right. I'll go. But I'll be back, and when you're clamer we can talk about it. Sleep on it, and I'll see you tomorrow.'

He turned to go, and she breathed a sigh of relief. Tomorrow she would be safe in New York, with thousands of miles between them, but she wasn't going to tell him that. He still didn't understand. She watched as he opened the door, holding her breath until he slowly stepped over the threshold.

He turned around, however, at the last minute, and gave her a long penetrating look. 'While you're thinking things over, Bianca,' he said calmly, 'you might ask yourself what the difference is between what I did in my films and what you did in the restaurant.'

With that he was gone, and the door closed firmly behind him. Trembling uncontrollably,

Bianca closed her eyes and blindly reached out a hand to brace herself against the wall. The encounter had shaken her badly. She had hoped to avoid it, but now that it was over, she could let go. Gradually, a sense of relief began to replace her distress. It was final, done.

She opened her eyes and reached down to pick up the sheets she had dropped. Still feeling a little weak and giddy, she slowly carried them back to the laundry room. Gerry's parting remark still on her mind, How could he compare the two situations? she thought in disgust. Her appearance at the restaurant and his suggestive roles in the films she had seen were not even remotely similar. And he had had the nerve to lose his temper over the episode with the drunk that night!

Angrily, she threw the sheets into the washing machine. She didn't want to leave even a trace of him or their lovemaking behind. She began to stride purposefully back to the bedroom when the telephone rang. She hesitated. Would he be calling her so soon? She just wouldn't answer it. Then she thought, it might be Tom. She'd better see. If it turned out to be Gerry, she'd just hang up on him. She went into the living room and picked up the receiver.

'Hello,' she said cautiously.

'Bianca,' came Tom's voice. 'I got your message. What's up?'

She sank down on to a nearby chair, so relieved to hear the familiar comforting voice that her knees were suddenly weak. Then she remembered that the reason she had called him that morning in the first place was to tell him she was getting married. What a farce! It seemed now like another lifetime instead of just a few hours ago.

Her mind raced. She'd have to tell Tom something. She needed his help, and owed him some explanation. Bracing herself, she drew in a deep breath to steady her nerves and plunged ahead.

'Tom, I've got to leave for New York right away, and I was wondering if you could look after a few things here for me.'

'What's wrong?' came his concerned voice. 'Not the family, I hope.'

'No, nothing like that. I'll explain later. Right now I've got a four o'clock plane to catch, and I need your help.'

'I'll be right over,' he said firmly.

'Oh, no, Tom. I couldn't ask you . . .'

'You're not asking,' he broke in. 'I'm telling you. Just sit tight. I'm only fifteen minutes away. There's plenty of time to get you to the airport by four.'

She hated to impose on him, but after they hung up she had to admit it did solve a lot of her problems. By the time she had put Laura's car in the garage and collected her suitcase, handbag and violin case, she heard Tom drive up in front. She ran out to meet him before he could get out of the car. She didn't want to run the slightest risk of Gerry seeing them and getting even an inkling of what was going on.

On the way to the airport she went down the list with Tom of what needed to be done in her absence, including calling Madame Tedescu, and he listened carefully while he drove, nodding and agreeing to each item. She could tell he was curious about the reason for her precipitate flight, but she wasn't ready yet to discuss it even with him. The humiliation and shame of it were still too raw for that.

'You know,' Tom said thoughtfully when she had finished, 'it occurs to me that if you don't think Laura would object, I could stay at the beach house.' He gave her a sidelong glance. 'It sounds as though your move back to New York is permanent.'

'Oh, yes,' she said stiffly, her eyes straight ahead. 'Quite permanent.' She didn't want to see the beach house or be reminded of it ever again. She glanced at Tom. 'That *is* an idea,' she said slowly. 'I'm sure Laura wouldn't mind. In fact, she'd be grateful. That's why I came in the first place, to take care of the house while she was in England. But don't you already have a place of your own?'

They were at the airport now, and Tom slowed down for the turn. 'I do,' he replied, his eyes on the oncoming traffic, 'but I've about had it with my roommate and would be glad of a place of my own. It's not a long drive from Malibu to the campus. I could easily commute.'

They had pulled up in front of the busy terminal. Tom put on the emergency brake and reached to turn off the ignition, but Bianca put a hand on his arm to stop him.

'No, Tom, don't come with me. I only have one bag and my fiddle. And I'd rather be alone.'

He turned to her. 'All right, Bianca, if that's what you want.' She started to get out of the car, but he reached out a restraining hand. She turned around. 'You're sure you don't want to tell me what's wrong, honey? Sometimes it helps. I don't like the way you look.'

'It's a long story, Tom,' she said. He would find

out soon enough, anyway, now that he was going to stay in Laura's house. Gerry would come looking for her. 'Do me one more favour, Tom. Please don't tell anyone where I am. Anyone at all.'

He nodded. 'Okay. But, Bianca, I wish you'd tell me what's going on. I only want to help.'

Tears came to her eyes then for the first time. It was exactly what she had been trying to avoid. She sensed instinctively that at this point any softness would be disastrous, that only the impetus of her anger would carry her through what she had to do. She didn't want to waver in her purpose or even think about what had happened until she was in New York and safely out of Gerry's reach.

She tried to smile. 'I just can't talk about it now, Tom,' she said in a wobbly voice. 'I'll call you soon and give you all the sordid details. I'm so grateful for all you've done.' Her voice threatened to break then, and she quickly got out of the car and reached in the back seat to retrieve her suitcase.

She gave him a little wave, then turned and began to walk towards the terminal. Her plane left in half an hour and she still had to check in her bag and pick up her ticket. There was no room now for regrets or second thoughts. There would be plenty of time later to cry, she thought as she went inside. Of that she could be certain.

CHAPTER NINE

BECAUSE of the time difference, it was the middle of the night before Bianca let herself wearily into her parent's apartment in New York. She had tried to sleep on the plane, but instead had sat painfully awake throughout the whole journey, dry-eyed, rigid, reliving every moment of the terrible day.

Even after she fell exhausted into bed in her old room, it was impossible to keep the hurtful images at bay. Gerry looming over her with his dark eyes full of desire, Gerry standing behind her soaping her slick body in the shower, his mouth and hands on her body, his voice in her ear murmuring words of love. Then the scene in her mind would flash abruptly to the sight of that same man on the enormous screen at the cinema, with the same mouth, hands and voice directed at a stranger, exactly as though she had stumbled upon him making love to another woman.

If only he had *told* me, she agonised over and over again as she tossed and turned in her bed. But what if he had? She would not have been able to resist going to one of his films eventually, and the same thing would have happened.

Finally, the tears came, and with them the blessed relief of a drug-like sleep at last. Her final thought as the darkness descended was of Tom's warning to her weeks ago that she might have to suffer to become a real musician and that the surest path to such suffering was an unhappy love affair.

She awoke the next day to the jangling ring of the telephone in the living room. For a moment, she was totally disorientated. Blinking in the sunlight coming in through the window, she glanced around the room in bewilderment. Then she remembered. She was back in New York. And with remembrance came the pain.

She shook her head, which seemed to be full of cotton wool and ached miserably. The telephone continued to ring. She groaned, slid out of bed, and stumbled into the living room, each step she took an insult to her pounding head. She lifted up the receiver and cleared her throat.

'Hello,' she said sleepily.

'Did I get you out of bed?' came Tom's cheerful voice. 'It's eleven o'clock here, and since you're three hours later, I thought it would be safe to call.'

Bianca sat down on the chair next to the telephone. She propped her elbow on the table and rested her forehead in her hand.

'It's okay, Tom. Is everything all right?'

'Well, that's why I'm calling,' he said slowly. He paused, then went on. 'Uh, Bianca, I stayed here at Laura's last night, and I had a visitor early this morning.' He paused again. 'He was quite upset.'

Yes, Bianca thought bitterly. He would be. The great sex symbol wasn't used to women fleeing *from* him. Immediately, she knew she wasn't being fair. Even though she despised Gerry now, he really had wanted to marry her after all.

'I'm sorry, Tom,' she said at last. 'I was afraid of that. I should have warned you, but I wasn't quite myself yesterday.'

'I knew that,' he replied hurriedly. 'Don't worry about it.'

'What happened?' she asked. 'Was it awful?'

He chuckled. 'Well, once I convinced him that hitting me wasn't going to make you suddenly materialise, it wasn't so bad.'

'You didn't tell him where I was,' she put in quickly.

'No. I hinted that you had gone to London to see Laura, but by that time I think the message got through to him that even if he found you it wouldn't do any good. I must say, Bianca,' he went on admiringly, 'you do seem to attract interesting men. That's two movie stars you've left behind in California with broken hearts. I'm Impressed. First Bruce Holloway, now Gerald Richards.'

'Tom, it isn't funny.' She was close to tears again. 'I didn't even know Bruce Holloway, and Gerry . . . Well, as it turns out, I didn't really know him, either.'

'Bianca,' he said softly, 'I don't know what happened or why you were so upset yesterday that you felt you had to run off like that, but he was really concerned about you. Actually, he seemed like a nice guy once he decided I wasn't the villain of the piece. You can imagine what he thought when I answered the door early this morning in my bathrobe.'

Men! Bianca thought bitterly. How they stick together! 'Tom,' she said in an even tone, 'have you ever seen one of his films?'

'No,' he replied slowly, 'I can't say I have. I'm not a movie-goer, and besides I don't think he's made one for several years.'

'Well, there's a Gerald Richards festival playing

now at a cinema in downtown Los Angeles. Go see it, and you'll understand just why I bolted out of there, why I can't marry him, why . . .' Her voice broke then, and she couldn't go on.

'Okay, okay, honey,' came Tom's soothing voice. 'I'm sorry. Let's just forget it. When he left here, he seemed to accept the fact that you were gone for good and it was really over between you. I don't think he'll bother you. Take my advice and concentrate on your music now. The hurt will pass, and you'll be a better musician for it, believe me.'

The days and weeks passed slowly. In time, Bianca's hurt and anger settled down into a dull ache. She was far from happy, but not quite so grindingly miserable, either. When the worst of the grief had passed, she took Tom's advice and concentrated hard on her music. It didn't seem to her that she was making any progress at all, but she kept doggedly at it, the hours she spent practising filling the long days and keeping thoughts of Gerry from consuming her.

He never contacted her in any way. As far as she knew he hadn't even tried to find her. Tom never mentioned him again, nor did she ever ask. As time went on, she had half-convinced herself that *he* had abandoned *her*, that his silence was further evidence of his shallow nature, that giving up so easily proved he'd never really loved her. It was all a game to him, she told herself. He'd been acting a part, and only seen her as a challenge, someone different from his usual bedmates. She even began to wonder if he had ever really intended to marry her; if that, too, hadn't been a deception, a manoeuvre to add her to his list of trophies.

The hot New York summer passed into an early Fall. By late September, the leaves in the park had begun to turn and there was a cool tang in the air. Soon it would be winter again. Bianca dreaded the thought. She'd been back home for three months. Surely Gerry would be gone from the beach by now. He'd said his friends were coming home from Japan in another month, and that was back in June.

She was playing now in a small chamber orchestra some old friends had recently organised, and gradually as they became known they were getting quite a few engagements. Between those concerts, in New York itself and in smaller outlying communities, and her gruelling hours of practice, she kept herself from moping. Her thoughts were never far from those months she had spent in Malibu, however, or from the man she had loved so completely. Even after all this time without seeing him or hearing his voice, his presence, if she let it, was almost as real to her as it had been then. It was a constant effort to keep thoughts of him out of her mind, and although time had dulled the pain, it hadn't dimmed her memories.

Gradually, too, she began to realise that she had behaved badly herself. All she could recall now were the good times, how much fun he was, how he had helped her get ready for her job at the restaurant, how much she had liked him, even aside from the strong physical bond between them. She remembered, too, the look in his eyes when she had called him that awful name and wished now that she could retract the hurtful words.

More than once she had been sorely tempted to call him, to apologise, to talk things over, perhaps begin again, but by that time it was too late. She didn't even know where he was. Besides, if he had really cared, he would have found her, called her, somehow got in touch with her.

No, it was too late. Surely in time the dull ache in her heart would be gone, she thought. There were other things in life. She had her music. And her memories.

Then, suddenly, in early October, New York seemed to be full of Gerald Richards. His book had been published and caused quite a sensation, not only for the publicity value of his movie fame, but for the shocking contents of the exposé of the Hollywood scene and its obvious literary merit. Everywhere Bianca looked, it seemed, there was that familiar face staring at her, in book shops, department stores, subway advertisements, news-stands. His publisher was milking the last drop of publicity out of the unusual situation.

Even the most severe literary critics seemed to take the book seriously. They had to, Bianca thought as she read the latest review one morning at breakfast in the apartment. It was a serious book. Beside the review in the morning newspaper was yet another photograph of the author, this one taken at the beach in Malibu. She recognised the exact spot. He was standing near the surf, the breeze ruffling through his dark hair, wearing a familiar pair of worn jeans and a knit shirt. His hands were shoved into his pockets, his eyes gazing directly into the camera. Barney was sitting at his feet, securely leashed and looking up at him adoringly.

Bianca caught her breath when she saw it, and tears stung her eyes. He looked so serious, she thought, but then isn't that what he said, that he was trying to be a more serious person? An agonising wave of sheer despair passed over her. This is what she had rejected and thrown away in her mindless, childish tantrum.

'Ex-Sex Symbol Turns Serious Novelist,' the caption read. And further on:

> Gerald Richards, former heart throb of a million panting women, has written a book, his first, that rips apart the Hollywood system of exploiting gullible young actors—male and female—in language that is stark and explicit, yet strangely poignant.

Bianca's eyes blurred. '*Ex*-Sex Symbol,' she thought. '*Former* heart throb.' Wasn't that exactly the point she had missed? The Gerry she knew, had fallen in love with, given herself to, promised to marry, was no more that stranger she had seen on the screen that day than she was the silly young girl who'd had a crush on Tom Schiffren at just about the same point in time.

She sat at the kitchen table, her head in her hands, the newspaper thrust aside, and groaned aloud. How could she have been so stupid, so blindly wanton as to throw away the one chance she had of real happiness? Tom was wrong. Music was no substitute for the man she loved. She'd tried. God, how she'd tried!

It was too late, she thought starkly, staring blankly into space. She'd really blown it. She turned back to the article and continued to read through the mist in her eyes.

It went on to praise the book, as well as the author's courage in relating experiences that must have been very painful to him. She came to the last paragraph:

> Mr Richards is currently on a whirlwind trip to the East Coast to promote his book and will appear at several book stores in the New York metropolitan area itself this week to sign autographs.

It went on to list the times and places of his appearances.

> He will also be interviewed tonight on PBS by the writer of this review. Tune in and see for yourself the apotheosis of sex-symbol into serious literary artist.

Bianca sat for a long time at the kitchen table, the newspaper in her hand, her breakfast forgotten, her thoughts churning. With all her heart she longed to get up from that table, go get dressed and run out to the first store where he was appearing that day. Just to look at him, she thought. She wouldn't speak to him or approach him in any way or let him know she was there. She only wanted to see him.

For a moment, she was strongly tempted to do just that and even half-rose from her chair. But she knew she couldn't. Just the thought of it made her knees grow weak, her pulse race. Slowly, she sank back down in her seat. She couldn't face it.

Somehow she managed to get through her normal day of household chores, grocery shopping, practising and rehearsing with the orchestra without succumbing to the temptation to go and see him, but it wasn't easy. Half a dozen times she found herself on the verge of looking up his schedule of appearances in the newspaper article and going there, but at the last minute her courage always failed her.

That night she sat huddled in her robe before the television set waiting for the interview to begin. Andrew Faraday was one of New York's most respected literary critics, and this was his regular programme. As she sat through the end of a nature programme and the station break, her heart pounded erratically and she sipped nervously at a glass of wine.

Then, suddenly, he was there on the small screen. He was sitting comfortably on a chair, totally at ease before the camera, his long legs slightly apart and bent at the knees, his elbows propped on the arms of the chair, his hands laced together under his chin. He was wearing a dark suit, white shirt and muted tie. She had never seen him in such formal, conservative dress before, and the sight of him took her breath away.

He was talking now, answering a question Andrew Faraday had apparently asked him. There was a serious expression on his face, and he gestured casually in the air with one hand as he spoke. Bianca made herself concentrate on the words.

'Naturally, I'm very pleased the book has been so well-received,' he was saying in a calm, relaxed tone. He smiled broadly, his even white teeth flashing against the dark tanned skin. 'Especially by the more serious critics.' He nodded courteously at his interviewer.

'Tell me, Mr Richards,' Faraday said, 'have you found your former—ah—reputation, shall we say, as a sex symbol to be an advantage or a hindrance in your new career as a writer?'

The smile faded. 'Quite definitely a hindrance,'

Gerry replied firmly. 'I realise it's possible that my book wouldn't have received the attention it has without the ballyhoo of my former film career, but I must accept the fact that I'll probably never live down that reputation you spoke of entirely, and it has been a handicap to me in many ways.'

'Are you speaking professionally or personally?'

Gerry hesitated for a moment. He appeared to be deep in thought. Then he said in a low voice, 'Both, I guess. It took me a long time to break out of the Hollywood mould, and even longer before I could get any publisher to take me seriously as a writer.' He waved a hand in the air. 'So the professional aspect was difficult enough. Personally, however, it's been a disaster.'

Faraday's ears perked up at that, and he leaned forward in his chair, 'Would you care to elaborate on that?' he asked silkily.

'No,' was Gerry's curt reply. Then he smiled again. 'We're here to talk about the book, remember?'

The rest of the programme was a blur to Bianca, a meaningless jumble of words. What did he mean by saying that his film reputation was a disaster to his personal life? Could it possibly be his relationship with her that he was referring to? A little ray of hope began to flicker in her breast.

Then she remembered the note of finality in his voice when he spoke of his personal life to the interviewer. Whatever it was, he seemed to have put it firmly out of his mind. And she remembered, too, that in all these months he had made no effort to contact her. She couldn't blame him, she thought, as she switched off the television set and walked slowly down the hall to her bedroom. Her parting words to him had been so brutal, her sudden disappearance so final, that it was no wonder he had put her out of his mind completely.

After a sleepless night, Bianca awoke the next morning with a resolution fixed firmly in her mind. Finally, she thought, she knew what she had to do.

After a light breakfast, she got up from the kitchen table and marched purposefully down the hall to get ready. She *had* to see him, even if it was only from a distance. She showered quickly, then dressed carefully in her bright red suit, hoping the cheerful colour would give her courage. She combed the mop of curly dark hair and tried to disguise the pallor of her face with a little blusher and a touch of lipstick. He wouldn't see her, but she knew the better she looked, the better she would feel.

When she was ready to go, she made a careful list of the book stores where he would be appearing that day. His first appearance was for ten o'clock at Brentano's, and it was after that now. She'd have to hurry. It was only a short walk away, and down on the street she set out in that direction. It was a crisp Fall day, bright with sunshine, and as she walked briskly along the crowded pavement, she realised that she felt better, more alive, than she had in all the months she'd been back in New York.

At last there was something she could *do*, she thought, some purpose to her life instead of the aimless drifting she'd been caught up in. She knew nothing would come of it. She had no intention of approaching him or even letting him know she was there. She just wanted to see him again.

At Brentano's there was a large crowd spilling

out on to the pavement. In the front window she could see a colourful display made up of several copies of Gerry's book stacked on a long table. There was also a large photograph of him placed prominently at one side of it. She craned her neck over the heads of the crowd and stood on tiptoes to get a better view of what was going on inside the store.

All she could see was the back of a dark head. He seemed to be seated at one end of the table, bent slightly forward. His face was not visible, but there was no doubt in her mind who it was. What should she do? The crowd seemed to be perfectly stationary, not moving at all. It might take hours to get inside, and even if she waited long enough to get a glimpse of him, what good would it do? She didn't want him to see her in any event.

At that moment there was a break in the crowd as it slowly shifted towards the door of the shop, and at the same time he turned his head slightly so that she could see his profile quite clearly. There was a fixed smile on his dark handsome face, the black hair was neatly combed and looked recently cut, the eyes hooded protectively. His head came clear around, then, and for a split second he seemed to be gazing directly at her. The dark eyes seemed to widen briefly in recognition, and the smile on his face faded.

Bianca's resolution suddenly faltered at the sight of him. With a little sob, she lowered her head, turned around and made her way through the crowd that had gathered behind her. She couldn't face it, she thought, as she began walking slowly back to the apartment.. Just the sight of him shook her to the depths of her being.

CHAPTER TEN

SHE stumbled blindly along, hardly looking to see where she was going, bumping into the scurrying passersby, the tears streaming freely down her face. She started across the street against a red light. A taxi driver yelled at her, and she stepped back up on the curb, dropping her handbag in her confusion. The contents spilled on the pavement, and as the unconcerned pedestrians hurried past her, she stooped down and with fumbling fingers began to retrieve her belongings.

Suddenly, she was conscious of someone stooping down next to her, a dark-clad pair of legs, bent knees straining against fine woollen material, then a large hand reaching out to pick up her wallet and place it inside her open bag.

She swiftly swivelled her head, startled, and found herself staring into a familiar pair of dark eyes. For a moment, all she could do was stare at him. A wave of dizziness passed over her.

'Gerry,' she breathed. 'You saw me.'

His face was only inches away from hers, so close that she could clearly see the fine stubble of his beard, the lines of strain around his eyes, a pulse throbbing along the firm curve of his jaw. The crowds continued to surge past them, cursing loudly at the pair stooping on the pavement, blocking traffic.

He looked away and finished stuffing things into her bag, then grasped her firmly by the arm and pulled her bodily over to a newspaper stand out of the line of traffic. She continued to stare dumbly at him, unable to take in the fact that he was actually there standing beside her.

'You—you followed me,' she finally managed to choke out.

He glared down at her with smouldering eyes. 'I ought to murder you on the spot,' he snarled. His hand was gripping her arm painfully.

'Gerry, I . . .' she began.

'Why did you come?' he barked at her.

She lowered her eyes. He hated her, she thought, and she didn't blame him. Then why had he followed her? Revenge? That wasn't in Gerry's make-up. She looked up at him, quailing before the grim expression on his face and the hard fury in his eyes.

'I didn't think you'd see me,' she said at last in a small voice. 'I just wanted to . . .' she faltered.

'To what?' he growled, giving her a shake. 'Did you leave something out last time we met? Have you learned some new names to call me?'

The tone of utter contempt in his voice finally undid her. With one stricken look at him, her face crumpled and she began to cry in earnest, great wracking sobs, like a hurt child. She was dimly aware of the interested glances of a few spectators, but she was beyond caring.

'No,' she blubbered. 'Not that.' Then, with her pride in tatters, she sniffled loudly and groaned. 'I came because I—I still care, and I just wanted one last look at you.'

For several long seconds he simply stared at her with an intense penetrating expression in his face, as though trying to pierce his way into her mind. A terrific battle seemed to be raging within him. Then, through her tears, she saw the hard mouth soften and the hand gripping her arm pulled her close against his chest. He stroked her hair and leaned down to place his cheek next to hers, his lips at her ear.

'God, Bianca, stop it.' he muttered. 'I can't stand to see you cry.'

A delicious warmth began to steal through her there in the shelter of his arms, and gradually the sobs subsided. She sighed happily. She may have lost him, she thought, but at least she had this one last moment of joy, the only one she'd experienced in all the months she'd been away from him.

He pulled away from her. 'Are you okay now?' he asked in a gruff voice.

She nodded and wiped her eyes with the back of her hand. 'Yes,' she replied. 'Fine.' He still wasn't smiling. She backed away from him and tried to compose herself. 'I'm sorry I made such a spectacle of myself,' she said stiffly. 'It was the shock of seeing you so suddenly like that.'

His hands were still on her shoulders. He removed them now and said, 'I've got to get back to Brentano's. Go home and wait for me. I'll come by as soon as I can get away.' He started to walk away from her into the crowd.

She called after him. 'But you don't know where I live.'

He turned back. 'Yes I do—my agent looked your address up for me. Wait for me.'

The next nine hours were the longest Bianca had ever spent in her life. She tried to eat lunch when she got back to the apartment, but the food stuck in her throat. She tried to practice, but all she produced was a toneless screeching. She called down to the doorman for the third time to make sure he understood that Mr Richards was to be sent right up when he arrived. She paced the apartment from one end to the other, wringing her hands, jumping when the telephone rang to inform her the evening rehearsal of the chamber orchestra had been called off, and going over and over again in her mind the meeting with Gerry that morning.

What did it mean? She agonised over every detail. He had been so distant, so stern. Not a flicker of a smile had once cracked that forbidding expression, He hated her. She knew that. Then why was he coming to see her?

Was he coming to see her? she finally wondered at seven o'clock that evening. He had told her to wait for him. Why? Was this his way of getting even with her? He'd known all along where she lived, yet had never once called or written. She didn't blame him after the way she'd treated him, but why did he want to see her now?

Finally, by eight o'clock, she was convinced that he didn't, that he had told her to wait for him simply to punish her, or get rid of her, that he'd never had any intention of coming to see her. She began to grow angry, and had half decided to leave the apartment, to just get out of that confining space, anywhere, when the doorbell rang.

Her anger instantly dissolved, and she flew to the door to answer it. Before she did, she made herself stop for a moment to collect herself. She ran a hand through her hair to give the wayward curls some semblance of order, knowing it was a futile effort, and smoothed out the red skirt of her suit. She would be calm, she told herself. Cool, calm and dignified. No more tears, no more scenes, no more hysterical outbursts. She arranged her features into a fixed, remote smile and opened the door, but when she saw him, the careful pose simply disappeared.

He was leaning there with one hand propped against the wall, his dark head slightly bent, and a look on his face of such ineffable strain and weariness that her heart melted within her. His suit was rumpled, his tie loosened, the top button of his white shirt undone, and his hair fell limply over his forehead.

He looked at her and sighed. 'Well,' he said wearily. 'Can I come in?'

She wanted to reach out and gather him into her arms, to hold his head to her breast, to comfort him, soothe him, *feed* him—anything, she thought, to ease that pinched look from his face.

Instead, she opened the door wider. 'Of course,' she said.

When he was inside, she shut the door and turned. His back was towards her. She watched as he took off his jacket, threw it over a chair, then stretched widely, the muscles of his shoulders and back rippling under the fine material of his shirt.

'God, what a day!' he muttered, slumping his shoulders forward, his arms hanging loosely at his sides.

'Would you like a drink?' she asked quietly, moving past him into the long living room.

'It would be manna from heaven,' he breathed fervently.

She went to the sideboard, her back to him, to pour them both a drink. She needed one herself. Under the cool exterior, her heart was pounding madly, and she was having trouble holding the bottle steady in her shaking fingers.

She could hear him moving around the room behind her, and when she turned to give him his drink, she saw that he was carefully inspecting the photographs and paintings along the walls and on the mantel of the fireplace. His long legs were apart, his fists resting lightly on his hips.

'So these are the famous Jamesons,' he remarked, turning to face her.

She handed him his drink. 'Yes,' she replied lightly. 'Quite a clan, isn't it?'

He took a long swallow of his drink and gazed steadily at her over the rim of the glass. 'You're all very much alike,' he commented. 'In looks, that is.'

'So I've been told.' There was a strained silence as they sipped their drinks. 'Are you hungry?' she asked finally.

He gave her a long look, drained his drink and set the empty glass down carefully on the mantelpiece. 'Yes,' he said at last. He moved across the few feet that separated them. 'For you.' His voice was husky, and at last he smiled. 'Put that drink down and I'll show you.'

With shaking fingers, she set her glass down, her eyes never leaving his, and the second it was out of her hand, his arms came around her. She slumped against him, holding him, their bodies pressed together so tightly she could scarcely breathe. They stood that way for several long moments, until finally Gerry's hand began to stroke her back.

'God, Bianca,' he breathed into her ear, 'you've just about driven me out of my mind.'

Still holding her firmly, he raised his head and glared darkly down at her. 'I should beat you within an inch of your life,' he bit out. 'Do you have any idea what I've been through these past few months?'

As she gazed up into his tormented eyes, she thought of her own suffering since she had left him. 'Yes,' she said quietly. 'I do.' She put a hand up and placed it on his cheek. 'I know now what a stupid, destructive thing I did, but Gerry, it was so terrible to see you up on that screen. It was exactly as though I was watching you make love to another woman in real life. The way you looked, the things you said and did.'

'It was only a *film*,' he ground out, his hands kneading her shoulders painfully. 'It *wasn't* real.'

'I know that now, but it *seemed* so real at the time. If only you'd told me, prepared me for it, it might not have come as such a shock.'

His hands gentled on her now, and he enfolded her tenderly in his arms, bringing her close up against him. 'I know, I know,' he murmured. 'I see now I handled it badly. It was all such a long time ago. I was only a kid, barely twenty, when that talent scout got hold of me out at Glacier. I just wanted to forget all about it. I should have realised you'd find out eventually, but I kept putting off telling you.' His hold on her tightened. 'I was so afraid of losing you, Bianca. You weren't like any woman I'd ever known before. I realise now that was the very reason I should have been more open with you right from the beginning.'

'Why weren't you, Gerry?' she asked. 'Why

didn't you tell me that first day on the beach who you were?'

He smiled bleakly. 'I was so damned glad—and surprised—that you didn't recognise me I just couldn't. That's why I was so rude to you that first day and why I tried to keep Flicka away from you.' The grin widened. 'It's not all a bed of roses being a sex symbol, you know.'

She thought about Bruce Holloway that night at the restaurant and the toll it took on him to deal with his fans. Then another thought occurred to her.

'That was the real reason for your disguise that night when you came to the restaurant, wasn't it? So you wouldn't be recognised.'

'Partly,' he admitted. 'Naturally, I didn't want anyone to know who I was, but I also didn't want you to find out I'd come there against your very strict orders.'

'Oh, Gerry,' she sighed, 'if only I'd known from the beginning, we could have saved ourselves so much grief.'

'I wonder,' he said musingly. 'It's possible that if you'd known who I was you would have run so fast I'd never have got to first base. And, after all, I did tell you my name that first night I came to your house. It's not my fault you're such a snob and have lived such a sheltered life that you'd never even heard of me. Knowing you, if you had, you probably would have run so fast I'd never have caught up with you.'

'Oh, I don't know,' she teased, flashing him a seductive smile. 'I seem to be more partial to sex symbols than I realised.' Her hand stroked down his cheek to the firm line of his jaw, the day-old beard rasping against her fingers. 'I was like putty in your hands.'

'Like hell,' he muttered, pulling her tightly against him. 'You were so standoffish I thought I'd never get near you.' He closed his eyes and heaved a deep sigh.

'Gerry, you're dead on your feet,' she said, pushing herself away from him a little. 'Why don't you have a shower and I'll fix you something to eat. It must have been a gruelling day for you.'

He released her and ran a hand through his dishevelled hair. 'Maybe you're right. I'm feeling pretty grubby.'

She led him to the bathroom. 'There are a zillion toothbrushes in the medicine chest,' she told him, 'and some disposable razors. One of the advantages of having brothers that simply show up from time to time. Mother is always prepared. Make yourself at home and I'll find a robe for you.'

When she came back with one of her father's old woollen bathrobes, Gerry was unbuttoning his shirt. She hung the robe on the hook in back of the door, trying hard not to look at him.

'I'll fix you some supper,' she mumbled. Out of the corner of her eye she saw the shirt come off and fall on the floor in a heap. Her hands began to tremble at the sight, her face and body warming dangerously. She heard the buckle of his belt as he undid it, the swish of the zipper on his trousers, and the heat running through her intensified.

'Aren't you going to wash my back?' he said in a low voice.

She had a flashing mental vision of him standing just behind her, stark naked, and it was all she could do not to turn around and throw herself into his arms.

'I don't think so,' she replied, making her voice as steady as possible. Then, as she slipped through the doorway and well out of his reach, she couldn't resist calling back to him over her shoulder. 'Maybe later.'

She could hear his laughter over the sound of running water as she hurried into the kitchen. Let him have his shower, she thought, as she rummaged in the cupboards looking for something to feed him. He liked tuna, she remembered, and there was plenty on hand. Pickles and potato chips, too, she recalled with a smile.

As she put on the coffee and mixed the tuna, listening to the splashing of the shower, she hummed softly to herself. For the first time in months, she felt really happy, really alive. Somehow she would forget that image of Gerry on the screen, or at least come to terms with it. She remembered what he had said that last day at Malibu when she had sent him away so brutally. There really wasn't that much difference between her performance at Rumania House in that skimpy costume and Gerry's acting on the screen, just as he'd pointed out. Both were only illusions, make-believe, and had nothing to do with the real person underneath the disguise.

When she finished the sandwiches, she wrapped them carefully in waxed paper and put them in the refrigerator. He might want a drink before he ate, or a rest. He had looked so tired. The water in the bathroom had been shut off some time ago, and he still hadn't appeared. She stood staring out of the kitchen window at the gathering darkness, every fibre of her being thrilling to the thought that Gerry was actually here, in the apartment, just a few feet away from her.

After waiting for him another five minutes she decided to check on him and went down the hall to the bathroom. The door was open, the towel he had used hung neatly on the rack. There was a used toothbrush and razor sitting on the counter near the wash basin, but otherwise there wasn't a trace of him. Then she noticed that his clothes were gone.

Instantly, she panicked. Had he left? Would he do that? She ran out into the hall to look for him. As she passed by her bedroom on the way to the living room, something caught her eye. She stopped short and looked inside. He was lying on her bed, one arm flung over his forehead, his eyes closed.

Her heart caught in her throat and she heaved a sigh of relief. Quietly, she tiptoed into the room and stood by the side of the bed gazing down at him in the dim light from the hall. He seemed to be deeply asleep, his chest rising and falling under the dark blue robe in a regular deep rhythm.

He is such a beautiful man, she thought, as she watched him. The sensuous mouth with its full underlip was relaxed. The long thick eyelashes rested on his high cheekbones, and the dark hair was still damp from the shower. The robe fell open a little at the neck, providing her a tantalising glimpse of his smooth muscular chest, and his strong, hair-roughened legs were visible from his knees to his bare feet below the robe.

I should cover him, she thought, and reached down to the foot of the bed for the rug folded there. But before she could reach it, she heard his voice.

'Bianca,' he said. She looked at him. His dark eyes glowed like black coals in the dimness, and held her startled gaze in his. 'Bianca,' he repeated.

'Yes, Gerry,' she replied breathlessly.

'Bianca, do you love me?' The low voice was hushed, expectant.

'Oh, yes, Gerry,' she breathed. 'I do love you so much.'

His hand reached out and clutched at hers. 'Then sit down here and show me,' he growled.

Slowly, she sank down on the bed, and grasping her arms, he pulled her down so that she was pressed against him, their faces only inches apart, the dark eyes boring into hers.

'Tell me again,' he ground out.

'I love you, Gerry,' she said softly. 'I always will.'

'And you'll marry me?' She nodded. 'And you won't ever leave me again?' She shook her head. With a low groan of satisfaction, his arms came around her and he held her to him so tightly that her breath was almost knocked out of her.

'God, Bianca,' he breathed into her ear, 'I love you to distraction. I was so afraid I'd lost you for good, that I'd never see you again, hold you like this.' The iron grip relaxed a little, and one hand came to the back of her head, running through the mop of dark curls, turning her face slightly so that he could kiss her.

The moment she felt that warm, sensual mouth under hers, all rational thought left her, and her one desire was for absolute surrender. Fire licked through her as the gentle pressure hardened, became more demanding. Her lips parted to allow his thrusting tongue entry, and they clung together, tasting and savouring each other at their banquet of love.

His hands moved possessively over her back, along her waist and hips, and then up over her ribs to settle on her breasts, already aching for his touch. Slowly, rhythmically, he kneaded the soft mounds until she moaned deep in her throat at the sensations those magic fingers aroused in her.

'Do you know what?' he gasped at last, his hands coming up to cradle her face, the fingers tracing every line and feature. 'You've got too many clothes on.'

She lifted slightly away from him and smiled down at him. 'I do believe you're right. What shall we do about it?'

For answer, he reached up and, his dark eyes never leaving hers, he slowly began to unbutton her blouse. With each downward motion his hand pressed against her, heightening her pleasure, until the last button was undone and he slid the blouse off her shoulders and over her arms.

She sat motionless before him and watched the gleam in his dark eyes grow brighter as they drank in her bare shoulders, the wispy flesh-coloured bra, the smooth flesh above the waistband of her skirt. He raised both his hands and ran the tips of his fingers very lightly over the hard points of her breasts, back and forth, then in a slow circular motion, until the ache became unbearable.

'Oh, Gerry, please,' she choked out, her eyes pleading.

He smiled and undid the clasp of her bra. As he pulled the straps down over her arms, his hands brushed against the burning naked flesh, and she closed her eyes in an agony of longing.

'You're so beautiful, darling,' she heard him murmur. She leaned over slightly so that her full breasts filled his waiting hands, then felt him rise up to place his moist lips over one taut nipple, his softly rasping tongue bathing it gently.

Finally, she couldn't bear the sweet torment a moment longer. She reached down and untied the dark robe, pushed it apart and ran her own hands down that beautiful body, from his broad shoulders, down his chest, his flat stomach, his rough thighs. His muscles and sinews rippled under the smooth skin, and soon he, too, was trembling.

He sat up abruptly and shrugged off the robe, then, kneeling before her, he unzipped her skirt and she raised her hips up so he could slide it off along with her last scrap of underwear. He laid her down on the bed and kissed her hungrily, lowering himself gently on top of her, his hard pulsing masculinity burning into her, his hands and mouth working their magic on her whole body until finally she could bear it no longer and she cried out.

'Now, Gerry! Oh, please, now!'

'Oh, yes, darling,' she heard him groan, and they were joined together at last. As they rode the crest of the wave together into an ecstatic climax, Bianca was certain she could hear music in her ears. Clinging to the man she loved, tumbling headlong over the precipice with him, the music seemed to soar with her to the end.

Heavenly music, she thought as she slowly wafted down from the pinnacle in Gerry's arms. Malibu music.